# TRUE LIFE

---

## JAYNE GRANT

To order additional copies of this book, contact:
**Bookwhip**
1-855-339-3589
https://www.bookwhip.com

# Chapter 1

T HE ESTATE FELT solemn…that is until you got inside. Lauren's voice filled the airwaves of the house. Vincent sought nothing more than blissful calming peace but saw no option of escape. Bond was in the office with him, learning the mechanisms of his father's business dealings. Bond was engrossed in a paper file and then contracted his shoulders which were rigid in posture. He then spoke aloud to Vincent. "Kind of overwhelming, isn't it?" Vincent jumped to Bond's view looking perplexed and a bit scared of his son's remark. Bond instantly sensed this. "No…I am not referring to the business." Vincent instantly lowered his tensed glare to him. "I am speaking of Lauren; can't we have the dogs chase her or something, and maybe if she gets tired…she'll be quiet."

In the confines of the room, Vincent made no eye contact with Bond. The boss stopped and moved to the side of Bond and then sat in the leather chair behind the desk, almost as if to reclaim his seniority. "There are two different locations in California that I have," his voice became frailer as he was finishing his last sentence. Bond composed himself and then instantly went to the chair opposite Vincent and sat there without making a sound. An unmoving air felt highly uncomfortable making him want to squirm, but he laid still and captive to his father. The boss bit his lip, and then opened and closed his mouth, then went into the speech.

"Of course," the boss stopped his speech and then moved his shoulders back, making it look that he was uncomfortable. Bond moved his head to the side lowering it. "Jane, being from the north region of the state in the San Francisco Bay area will want to stay there." But a brief pause was made by him and then he recaptured his speech. He took his open hand to his mouth and then mumbled words that Bond could not understand. In the countless years of this business, Bond more than knew when to be quiet and when to wait. And this was one of those times. "Ideally, I do want to go to the l.A. area as there are many business contacts there."

Bond wondered - it was more than apparent that the boss, his dad, wanted Chris to go to CA, "He was the boss" why didn't he just say this to Chris? Then in the next breath Bond knew the answer: it was his job to drop this news. Awkward silence again traveled through the room. Bond then rolled his tongue over the top of his lip, then breathed out and moved his mouth to the side. He looked into the eyes of his father, still hearing nothing. An overwhelming silence again filled the air. Bond could more than sense that his father became burdened with sorrow that Chris was going to leave. Bond opened his mouth to say something comforting to his dad but found no words.

The boss rose up from the comfort of the chair then had a balance problem as he tried to walk forward to the side. He immediately placed his hand on the side of the desk for support and balance. Bond instantly was ready to jump to the needs of his dad. The boss made a side vision of him then paused now secure in his stance but said nothing to Bond. He moved slowly out the door of the room and told Bond that he needed to rest. This was now the only time that Bond did not follow him out and to his room, as he tried to weigh everything that was now his job.

Bond crossed his arms, and then opened his mouth, taking in some air, then took his hand to his mouth and breathed in more. Before he even knew it- he was in his father's room, checking on him. Vincent was on his side with his legs curled up almost in the fetal position. An open bottle of pills laid on the nightstand next to a half-drunk glass of water. Bond went to his father's side. He instantly covered him with a blanket then reached for the pills, standing them up and put the cap back on. He whispered out,

"I do love you…dad, this has just been a lot to take in lately." After making this comment, he left the room and closed the door.

Standing against the window and looking out to the beach he said aloud, "A nice jog on the beach running from the waves would feel really good right now, a release. But then, I do still have the fear that Jane will find me and try something. I have to…she has to stay away from me, especially now." He then pulled his lips inside his mouth, contracted his shoulders then loosened them as a shiver went down his body. He thought in his mind, *I have never felt loneliness until now. He* stood back from the window, then returned his body to a guard in motion and left the room.

Inside Jane's room, she and Chris left the steamy bathroom each wearing a white terry cloth bathrobe. Chris went to the table and pulled a chair out, motioning for Jane to sit, he then sat as well. She smiled at him. He then relaxed his body leaning back in the chair. He stopped and pointed to her, "Have a lot of catching up to do. Jane, tell me about your life." He wanted to hear everything. She told him where she lived and what her name was and her job, the neighbors, her daughter's friends, and her boyfriend. etc. Instead of being taken back by this, he relished it.

All the time in listening to her he knew very clear that he could not tell her anything that he had done. He did stand up and opened a bottle of 2013 Domaine Morgan red Beaujolais. For the first time since she opened her mouth to speak, she took a long breath then stopped her speech to savor this impeccable wine. "Oh, Chris, I want nothing more than to be with you forever." He took hold of her glass, and then gently put it down. He then took her hand and motioned her up, then gently pulled her into a deep hug where they could literally feel each other breathing. If ever there was such a perfect moment, she couldn't imagine.

Bond went to his bedroom - something he usually never did unless to sleep or change clothes. He looked at the end corner of the queen size bed, it was already made. He stared at it as he had never seen it before. It was brushed cotton, a dull pale orange with small white raised dots. Only then did he reach down to it and felt the upraised cotton dots. He thought it would be uncomfortable to rest on, but then he thought this went well with his job; seeing the idea of comfort, but not taking it until you knew that it was absolutely safe. He bent one knee down and turned to look like he was assuming either a yoga position or a karate move. In a dormant unmoving stance in an instant, he jumped turning around and jumped to his backside. He slowly rose up from this movement, and then said softly aloud, "How can you put a jaguar behind a desk, cage him?" he rolled his lips with his tongue, then felt for his keys in his pocket and left the room and the house.

He walked in instant pre-planned steps to the open garage. Their mechanic was there working on the vehicles. He made a quick swipe looking over each one, then proceeding to the white Ferrari; he got into it so fast you barely had a chance to see him get in. The engine was started. He was in the motion of backing out of the garage when the mechanic ran to him and yelled out. He heard the talk but did not listen to the words. While waiting for the automatic gate to open, he saw the mechanic running for him. The only thing in his mind was pure escape. He almost floored the pedal and drove to the west side of the estate, then took a side road seeing only small homes to each side of the street. He did then lower his foot on the pedal and slow down significantly in speed.

He heard a beeping sound that came from the dashboard. The car lost power, he thought - *what am I doing wrong?* he looked onto the dashboard then instantly back up to his driver's view and slammed on the brakes. A metal trash can was to his right and a woman standing behind, and to the side of it in her driveway calmly watching him. He looked to her then back down to the dash and slowly turned off the engine breathing out, looking like a football player who just lost the championship game of the season. He opened the driver's door and got out of the car. This middle age brown-haired blue-eyed woman walked over and stood just three feet from him. "Looks like you've got problems there. Out of gas, maybe?" he looked at her and smiled, then put his head down and quietly said, yes. She snickered and then he did too. She motioned for him to come inside her home, she just made a pot of coffee. He followed her into her home. Her pet bulldog barked at the door; she quietly told it to quiet and it did and resumed resting on a floor pillow. Bond then thought this was the perfect set-up to get him and how he was following it right to the letter. There was just something in his trained professional mind that told him that this was okay…he was safe - something that he sought forever at that moment.

Sitting down at the small round dark wood table, he breathed out and smiled, reaching for the cup of coffee she was about to place on the table. "You had better wait for me to put it down before you take it. I don't want to burn you." He nodded, and then leaned further back while she did this. He took a sip then made an affirmative remark to the good taste of her coffee. She sat back observing him and spoke out you are welcome. He took another sip then asked her, "Do you always…" If I don't, who will? What were you thinking about when you ran out of gas? He took his hand to his thighs and rubbed them up and down. Oh, just a lot of changes. He scratched the side of his face then looked over to her, wanting to get the attention from him. He asked her what she was doing there looking so calm. She replied, "Oh, thinking about the difference between neutrons, protons and electrons." He then laughed.

"Are you a teacher? A science teacher, maybe." She took her hand to her mouth, covered it then let it down to the table. "No, I thought of teaching for a while, but never pursued it. I've worked here and there at a lot of different jobs. Now I am a preservationist at one of the big hotels here on the island. And what about you, driving that car and looking so debonair, a spy maybe?" he choked and had a time keeping the sip of coffee in his mouth, then after doing so, he let out a smirk, "Yeah, something like that." She laughed then nodded her head, "Okay mystery man. Driving that car, that is it, you are a car salesman." He relaxed letting his hand open on his thigh then breathed out.

"I am sorry to interrupt this nice time that we are having, but seriously, I have to get to work. But what about my car?... I'll call my family and they'll," he stopped his speech, not wanting to say anything further on his family. "They'll come and get you, your wife maybe?"

"No, I'm not married." Her eyes lit up hearing this from him. He saw this and then responded, "Are you?"

"No, I am divorced." In a motion of getting up, he responded back the same here. She took her purse and jacket from the side counter, then he and the dog followed her out of the house. He waited as she locked the door and then before going to her SUV, she handed him a small card with her cell number on it. He took it then viewed it smiling to her. "You didn't think that I was going to let you get away, did you? Mr. Spy." He laughed then said, "name's Bond." fitting, she moved her head down, "My name is Laurie, then, my dog's name is lady, you have a nice day." He stepped back and grabbed his posture, then thanked her for the coffee and the help. She nodded from her car as she drove away. In just seconds after making the call, he saw a family car stop and pick him up. He was very surprised seeing that it was Chris who was driving to his rescue. Inside the car, they each made a nod to each other. Chris opened the conversation, "It's been a long time."

"Yes, it has. It is nice you being here again, and thanks for…" "Hey, you don't have to say anything more. The place that you were in, a girlfriend maybe. That's nice, you need one." Bond was surprised to hear this from Chris. He closed his mouth then leaned back in the seat, then opened his mouth and said "maybe."

Inside the main house at the estate, they went into their father's bedroom. They were surprised not to see him in the bed. Chris ran in the bathroom, in only seconds he rushed out. Chris nodded to Bond and they both raced through the house looking for Vincent. Fear shadowed Bond's mind. Then with an overwhelming breath out, both relaxed their rigid composure seeing Vincent sitting behind the desk in his office. Vincent looked up to him in a locked silent stare. They each walked forward to him and sat down in chairs opposite to him at the desk, they both did this in complete silence and unison.

It seems that I thought that only the father remained - I just found out there are more. They aren't actual family members, but they work for him and follow him like family. "Boys, the fun is not over… yet. Chris, you will not be going to California after all. Both of you will be going to Vegas - Las Vegas, Nevada. Chris, you, and your wife- family will be making this your new…home. This is where they are dealing with now. Bond, you will be going to stake out the area so that we know what and where we are working." Both Bond and Chris noticed and uplifted composure to Vincent. Bond thought of his father's safety being that he will be alone on the island with the two of them being gone. Vincent instantly picked up on this. "I've already arranged for other members of our organization to be here, protecting me. This will be a solo trip just the two of you. Go and tell Jane and blabbermouth the daughter. Just tell them that the two of you must go away, but DO NOT tell them Vegas." He closed his eyes and nodded his head. They both knew that this meant to leave and went outside to the girls.

Jane and Lauren were sitting on a chaise lounge. Now stopped four feet from the two girls, they were surprised that the two of them didn't look up to them. Bond saw that they were both doing some sort of sewing which really surprised him. Jane lifted her head to Chris and smiled, then briefly looked to Bond and did the same. She noted the questioning glare that they were giving them. She stopped holding a knitting needle. "We are working on knitting, a project so to speak." Chris and Bond looked at each other as if questioning which one of them was going to speak first to the girls about their trip.

Bond nodded to Chris to do the talking. Chris gave a side stare to Bond and then proceeding into verse.

"We just talked to Vincent, and it seems that there have been some changes that we are going to follow." He immediately noticed a quick questioning expression and saw that Lauren didn't pay much attention as to even change her expression or the course of her knitting. He took a brief side view of Bond showing no emotion. Then told the now worried Jane that he and Bond were just going to Los Angeles to check things out before making the move, and that this was just being done to make sure of their safety there. Jane moved her head back down to the knitting and made no verbal comment. This action surprised both Chris and Bond as they gave a side glare to each other. Seeing the two girls looking down, he raised his shoulders and then Bond did also as they both turned and walked back to the house.

After closing the door, he stopped and looked at Chris who also stopped and showed a look of concern as to what Bond was going to say. "Did you ever wonder if they already know something?" Chris laughed. "Yeah, they are women." Then the two of them laughed as they walked away. Parting ways to go pack for the trip, it had been a long time since they worked together and both of them looked forward to this.

The dinner hour came sooner than either of them wanted to see. Before they knew it, they were all at the table eating and making small talk through the course of the meal. An occasional snide remark came from Lauren's mouth to raze Bond. She savored the end of the meal so that she could return upstairs to her room to text to her friends. Even Jane was surprised at how well Lauren was taking this change of being there on the island. Lauren already has gone and the three men remained seated. Jane got up and motioned for Chris to return upstairs with her. He shook his head from side to side to her. The boss picked up on this and then told Jane that the three of them were going to have some "man" conversation, signaling for her to leave. She more than hesitantly left. Vincent then motioned for a guard; Bond started up from his chair thinking something wrong. The boss moved his hand down signaling for Bond to return to his seat. The guard then came back and whispered to Vincent that indeed Jane had left.

"You boys know the usual course of action. California is a no; the new place is in Vegas. Las Vegas. You will come into people who will ask you why you are there and where you are going to stay. As both of you will be traveling a commercial jet there. You each pick one of your aliases. You'll act as you just became friends on your trip there. The Bellagio is where you will stay. You'll check-in and have an adjoining room and you will each go in. But I will have someone go back into these rooms after each one of you has left your rooms. They do keep track of guests' room doors opening and closing. This way when and if someone does catch on to you, they'll think you are in the room."

"You will be staying at a friend's residence that I do have there. Don't worry about your belongings; fake identical bags will go to the hotel and your bags will go separately to his residence." Bond wanted to jump into the conversation and ask him where and who with, but then he thought Chris would do this, but he didn't, he just kept quiet. They were told more of what to expect and what to do when and after they got there. There was reassurance felt by each that they'd be doing this job together so to speak. Chris just seemed much more composed which Bond felt a bit leery of. But when he thought of what Chris had done, he felt comfortable.

The boys left. Vincent sat back still in his chair, feeling the happiness run through his veins knowing he was back in the game. He slept better than usual awakening with the sun as he did most every day. In his now older years of life, he experienced the body slowing down, but somehow, just somehow, it was easier today.

Chris and Bond each proceeded to pack for this journey. While packing Bond thought to himself, well at least I don't have to worry of passports or which language I'll be using. Chris laid out his luggage over the bed and then systematically as though a robot packed all the bags with every item needed. At the bottom of the stairs, the two of them unknowingly bumped into each other and Bond was the first to react making a soft grunt; then stepping back facing to the floor, Chris said nothing, and he just remained in his stance unmoved and quiet. It was an awkward moment for both of them. The sound of the opening of the front door and two guards going in the house and taking their bags away released the tension.

Again, in complete unison the two of them proceeded to the dark color SUV. Chris sat in the back on the driver's side and Bond sat in the back of the passenger side. The engine started and it seemed that they're both relaxed to even the sound of the motion of the vehicle. Turning out of the gate of the estate, they looked at each other then rolled their hands out to the other to coordinate the time of their watches. It was a nice clear day-Chris put his sunglasses on which seemed to only be looking ahead. Bond made note of everything that they passed on his side of the SUV. He quickly moved his head even closer to the side window observing something. Chris made note of this but said nothing.

It was a small light stained wood coffee shop, a glass door in the middle of it and a side employee entrance on the east side of it to the left. A small SUV was parked there to the side of it and much to Bond's surprise the mystery woman that he had just met, Laurie was there. He saw in that brief moment going by that she unlocked the side door and went in holding a bag. Chris further picked up on his brother's questioning view of this. Chris then asked Bond if everything was okay. Bond shook himself back to a relaxed composure and then said "yes". And the conversation ended with Chris smiling.

They got their bags out the SUV while the engine was still on, a baggage attendant went to them and Chris instantly shook his head no, Chris to the left and Bond to the right. Once inside, they converged side by side as unplanned. Chris's cell phone then beeped and he left to the back of where he stood next to the side of Bond to take the call. Bond only looked straight ahead and walked closer to the check-in counter; while he was in the motion of doing this his cell phone went off. He retraced his footprints and then stood only 10 feet from where Chris stood to check on the information that he was just texted.

They both read through their messages and Chris turned his head up in the direction of Bond though not directly at him and raised his left eyebrow. Bond saw this and then faked a sneeze looking at Chris's view.

They then proceeded to the ticket counter. Halfway through the motion there, Bond again started coughing and then turned away from the direction of the ticket counter and instead, he went to one of the many gift shops at the airport and bought a pack of cough drops. After paying for them, he waited until he was back in total view of the airport before he opened it and took one out then started sucking on it. The strong flavor of the lozenge caused him to cough even more. He did a vertical 90-degree sweep for Chris and didn't see him. The only thing he thought of left to go went to the gate hoping that Chris was alright. He got his paper ticket and then proceeded to the assigned gate.

In scoping out a place to sit, he saw almost all of the chair banks were already full of people and any empty ones had passengers' bags, purses or items on, Bond thought, "Well I guess they are trying to get some sort of space to enjoy before being herded onto the crowded squeezed airplane flight." Before entering the boarding gate, he saw Chris at the sidebar with a woman to each side of him flirting. Bond looked at him and then opened his eyes wider then pulled back his head breathing out. Chris smiled at each of these women then took another sip of his drink, cracked a joke which they all laughed, and then he walked to the gate as it was now boarding.

Everyone on the flight now is seated and while waiting for the take-off, the stewardesses made one final trip up and down the aisles making sure that everything was to code. Both Bond and Chris were seated for the second to the last row on the left-hand side of the plane. The last seat row behind them was empty as the chair bank was covered and an out of order sign was placed on it. Chris had the seat next to the window and Bond has the aisle seat. The middle seat was wet; somehow, a large container of liquid was spilled there, so it was not usable. The last stewardess making exception saw this then tried to dry the seat; being unable to she taped over it, so no one would try to sit there.

Take off was a bit bumpy, Chris contracted his body and swallowed hard. Bond thought - serves you right for having a drink before take-off. An hour or so into the flight they were served drinks, Bond opted for water While Chris had nothing as he was asleep. Bond opened a paperback novel he had brought along for reading on this flight, a Dean

Koontz novel. He had notes of needed info about this trip in it. The flight attendant saw this and asked him which one it was. He pulled back surprised, and then relaxed his composure looking sideways at it, and reading the title-Strangers, he then told her that. She replied she hadn't read that one yet, and then asked him if it was good. He replied, "Of course, it is well." He stopped then tilted the book closer to him, "It is Dean," she smiled then proceeded back up the aisle.

The plane arrived and all the passengers were exiting the plane at the Las Vegas airport. Each exited the plane according to how they were able to squeeze themselves out of a tightly woven ball. Where to find a room, and where to stand without getting pushed or coughed on. Outside in the terminal, Bond instantly went to the right and then relaxed against a planter, while looking at a piece of paper displaying various hotels, making he seem like the utmost tourist. Chris stood to the side of where the line of people exiting the plane. He stopped in his motion like he was looking for someone who would meet him there to pick him up. All of the passengers of the plane had exited, and then Chris went to the restrooms that were ahead to the left. A cleaning cart with two janitors had closed off the men's restroom; there was a plastic sign on the floor that said closed cleaning. One of the men came out and moved the sign. The other man came out and got rolls of paper towels. Both janitors went back in. Then Chris almost ran in looking like it was an emergency to get to stall in time. Bond tilted his body back closing the pamphlet, and almost fell, he caught himself. Then laughed feeling embarrassed and then went to the restroom.

Approximately 10 minutes later the janitors wheeled the cart out of the front of the restroom and turned it to the left making the way clear to the restrooms. Both Bond and Chris then exited the restrooms and turned to the signs reading baggage and taxi. They were because of each other, but never passed an eye to the other. Now outside, Bond has gone to one of the airport workers and seemed to ask him something. Bond then turned away smiling and ran for a limo as the taxi line was just too long. Chris waved down a white Prius where a dark-haired woman wearing a navy scarf tied around her neck and a beach weave hat waved him down. He ran to her, hugged, and then got in the car.

A white service van each with banners to the side of van read land's cleaning service, one followed Bond in the limo and Chris in the Prius. All three vehicles were now on the freeway though distanced from each other. Now entering the hotel leave off, Bond got out of the limo, paid, and tipped the driver then ran inside to check-in. The white cleaning van went to the side of the passenger drop off and four men wearing dark blue uniforms then ran out of the van then drove off behind the hotel.

Chris exited then waved goodbye to the woman that drove him there and he entered the hotel making no note of the uniformed men running into the hotel. In the crowded entrance, each got lost in the crowd. The uniformed men watched- two of them on each side of the crowd. A sudden rush of people rallied through the front entrance throwing the guards off focus. By the time that the guards were able to regain their view, they saw each of them enter an elevator. Two jumped in the very next one to open, the other stayed to view the floor number that it would stop at. The two of them exited the elevator to the 11$^{th}$ floor and then ran down the hall where one still got a glimpse of the boys.

The door to each room closed, rooms right next to the other. The men then stopped at the closed doors looking quite perplexed at what to do next. In just a few moments they left, with the satisfaction of knowing where the two Mondello's were.

Both of the brothers now inside the hotel rooms made no note of the adjoining door. Chris threw off his jacket landing on the bed then looked at his watch. Bond hung his jacket up in the closet then laid his bag on the dresser. In a choreographed movement, each went to the sliding glass door of their separate rooms. The first thing that Bond noted was no beach as this was the view that he was used to seeing. Chris locked his body in view then relaxed his composure. There was a window-washing ladder and steel 4 by 4 dolly right outside of the right of both rooms. No other window was to the side as the building turned at that point and was just cement after Chris' room. Bond's room the left of his, as an invisible silent countdown happened each of then opened the sliding doors in unison and stepped onto the platform. As this happened, 2 men looking for them each went inside their separate rooms as the platform was lowered to the ground.

At the side opening of the walkway where it became larger in the cemented area off the edge of the grass flowered walkway, a white van with an open back door awaited. Both Chris and Bond jumped in the back of the white van, then the back door closed and then it traveled away from the hotel grounds and on to traffic in the street. As the van drove away the side of the van came into view, lands Cleaning Service. The white van that was to have picked them up was to the front side of the entrance of the hotel. Both of them looked to the other raising their eyebrows to each other both in shock and panic.

The correct white van was now on the tail of the cleaning van. Bond bent over coughing. Chris picked up on him and then reached for something in his inside pant leg. As he did this, he faked a cough as well. As in the case of monkey see monkey do, the two in front of the van started coughing. Bond then took a rag from Chris's hand and each of them sprang forward and covered the faces of the driver and passenger of the van. In doing this, the van lost control and veered to the right side and off of the road. Then it went face first into tall heavy bushes lining the side of the road. The driver and the other immediately started coughing and with each breathe that they tried to grab, it became more difficult to move, slowing them down as delirium seemed to take over.

The sound of the van now parked behind them sounds intensified, the running footsteps seemed to amplify as they came closer to them. Each of the front doors was opened and then two uniformed men grabbed the shaking bodies and pushed them out of the cleaning van. Chris then leaned back into the back seat and kicked open the back doors and both he and Bond jumped out of the van then nodded to the two men that helped form the old van as they got in the new van. Inside the men, all nodded to the other, and then the driver apologized about that mix-up. And replied, "Chloroform?" Chris simply nodded and then Bond turned his face from the side and softly said, "Okay." He swallowed hard then looked to Chris, "The hunt is on." Chris sat motionlessly and then replied, "Again." They looked at each other, reaching to the other's side hand, then held it tight for 10 seconds and then released it.

Back at the estate, Vincent walked in the front door, eyeing it, then retraced his steps back to the office but didn't go in. his head guard how he now called by his first name, Fred, informed him that the girls (Jane and Lauren) were now at her former apartment in the Silicon Valley and packing their belongings, then they would be coming back to the estate as their new residency was not secure yet. Vincent nodded. Then he moved like repositioning his stance in waiting to hear something more. Fred picked up on this and then told him that his friend is flying into the Island that day and he would be there in the evening. Vincent further nodded. He then proceeded to the living room couch and closed the long flowing drapes closed, blocking the view of the outside. The room became darker, but the knowledge of the day-time hours remained in his mind. He got up for only a brief moment to turn on the stereo, then relaxed his rigid composure hearing the rhythmic sound of Mozart. He sat there undisturbed as the day turned into the evening hours.

Hearing the sound of the front doorbell ring rattled him awake. He opened his eyes but remained locked there on the couch. He only motion that he did make was taking hold of the remote to open the drapes, the room only slightly lit up from the outside lights that were no visible. He adjusted his eyes then straightened his back still sitting. He could hear talking, and then recognizing a certain voice he smiled, relaxed his body, and took a stance from the couch. Jonathan walked toward him smiling and became faster in his walk to get to Vincent. He was a tall, wispy brown-haired gentleman with just a hint of gray showing on the hair at the side of his face. He was in very good form, physically. The two embraced each other in a tight hug, then released standing only two feet apart and smiled to each other speaking. Then they both stopped leaving the floors open to the other. Laughter then filled the air and Jonathan opened the conversation.

He had a slight Irish accent which added to his charm. "It has been years! I am glad that you called. You made it sound like rather an emergency, so I got on the first jet here. What is it?" Vincent breathed out then took his hand to his heart and proceeded to tell him of all of the latest occurrences and how his sons were now in Las Vegas. Jonathan nodded his head to him and gave him a look back like he had feelings for everything that the boss had just told him. Vincent picked up on this and was thankful. He then got up as his guard came to his side. The boss quietly said some words to the guard as Jonathan observed but said nothing making himself comfortable on the couch. An iced glass of Jameson was just handed to each one of them. Jonathan raised his glass to Vincent's clanking it in a toast but said no words, only a smile.

"You know, Vincent this seems rather planned but believe it is not, right now I am in the process of actually moving to where you speak of, Vegas, Las Vegas that is, and no I am not just saying this, it is the truth. Your sons, Bond and..." Vincent replied, "Chris." Jonathan nodded his head to him, "That's right, Chris. Well, it looks like they could or might need my help?" Vincent nodded his head and then they took another toast, then headed to the table for the evening meal.

Stories and laughter filled the air of the dining room through the course of the meal. Jonathan's eyes reflected from the overhead light bringing attention to his once broken nose that never seemed to realign itself, from an old sports injury. Vincent thought this added to his character. Both of them left the dining room and turned in for the night.

Jonathan referred to where everything was in his guest room. Now relaxed in his light gray pajamas, he circled the room while rhythmically breathing. He stopped and scratched his elbow, then sat at the left corner of the bed. He raised his right hand to his chin, then closed his eyes and reopened them expressing a concern as if he'd remembered all words of a speech that had to recite. He then took a deep breath in and rose to his feet.

"This will be something new...It has just been something that I have been waiting for.... Thank you." He then pulled the covers down and got into bed. He reached over and turned the lamp off, then rolled to his side and made heavy breathes out and then turned his body under the covers. In a quick motion he got out of bed, saying aloud, "This is not going to work." He went to the right side of the bed, pulled open the covers and got back into bed. "Yes, this is my side." And in just five minutes later a light snore came from his sleeping body.

# Chapter 2

NOW DRIVING DOWN the 95 South freeways in Vegas, they both noted the heavy traffic there. Chris spoke aloud, "This reminds me of l.A." The driver countered back, "A lot of people have moved here lately; it is defiantly not the sleepy town it once was." Bond just listened while realigning his body in the seat looking for comfort. Chris noted this then replied, "It is not the seat that is making you uncomfortable, it is being in a new place to call home." Bond slightly opened his mouth then ran his tongue against the side of his bottom left teeth and then ran it over his front teeth, opened then closed this lips and bit down. He moved his head to the right and took his left hand and moved up and down the top of his head, then swirled his open hand in front of him to see what it held, nothing. The driver watched this in the rear-view mirror then replied, "Once you get used to life here, you'll feel different."

Now off the freeway and being off five different side roads, they pulled into a gated housing community. They stopped at the end of one of the streets there; Bond took a sweeping "spy" view then looked to Chris who only looked to the left side of the van. There on the left side of what looked like a dead-end road with no getaway, there was a small code box four feet tall. The driver entered a code and then, a large boulder in front of the van moved to the side. The driver waited for it to stop and then drove in. Chris smiled, "Good camouflage." Bond just motioned to Chris tilting his head.

Now at the top of a plateau, they could see the two-story white mansion and the manicured grounds and swimming pool. They all got out of the parked van on the left side of the circular driveway. A blonde hair, tan skin middle-aged man wearing a loose tropical shirt and white pants with a sailor's hat, and gold-rimmed sunglasses approached. A red cocker, spaniel to his side that slowly ran to them was wagging its tail. The driver went to this man first as the two men stood to the side while they said their hellos and shook hands.

"Boys, I'd like to introduce you to Dave Sands." They each walked forward to him, but Bond shows some hesitation, and then shook his hand after Chris did. Dave could see this in Bond, and then said, "Relax, neither the dog nor I bite. And the dog's name is ruffs." After Bond did shake his hand, he looked at him questionably, "Weren't you a spy in a San Francisco TV show? Years back." Dave started to loosen up, but then when he heard, "years ago" he straightened his stance. "I was a cop - a detective, not a spy. Will let's go in." At that moment a cloudburst was heard, and it started pouring rain. All of them quicken their pace to enter the front door of the home. Bond looked highly uncomfortable trying to wipe the cold wetness off of his shirt. Dave saw this and told him that it would be dry in a minute, and it was. He then explained that there in Vegas they got short bursts of heavy rain all year long and when it did happen, it was welcome.

Inside the home, the massive center living room was all in white - white furniture, white walls, and white carpet but the only thing that wasn't white was a glass top coffee table. Bond wanted to walk away from it which he did, leaving the others still standing at the front door. He went straight forward to the glass wall that looked out to the Las Vegas Valley. It was quite a view. Dave picked up on this and then nodded to the gentlemen at the door and walked to Bond standing at the glass wall. "It looks okay now but wait until you see it at night with all the lights," he then smirked as he closed his dialogue. Under his breath Bond thought, "Yeah, but no beach". He tilted his head and nodded to Dave. "Ruffs" the dog came to his side and tilted his head up to him waiting for direction. "You go and show Chris his room and Bond...is it? Bond, your room is right across the hallway from your brothers." Ruffs then barked and started in direction of their rooms.

Chris' room looked out to the view of the valley. Once inside the room, he did think it odd that it was not in white as the other part of the house that he saw. It was in gold and blue and walnut stained headboard over a King bed and night tables. An enclosed bath was in the right with the entrance to the right near the window. Bond sheepishly opened the door to his room. He scoped it out before setting foot inside. It wasn't a small room, but not large by any means. The colors were the same as his brother's bedroom, the one big exception was no view and a small window that looked out to the front of the estate as you drive in, no view. Bond walked forward and dropped his bag on the floor on the way on the bed. He sat on the corner of it then rubbed the side of his neck and smiled, "I like it."

After they unpacked and got settled in their rooms, they met Dave outside on the deck overlooking the valley. Dave sat looking north and Chris in the middle looking at the view of the valley and Bond to the side of him. Evening was settling in, and the lights were now vaguely visible. Dave was settled back and now had his dark glasses off and held a cocktail. The boys were offered one; Chris had a martini and Bond a glass of ice water. Dave opened the dialogue looking to Bond, "If you're wondering about the dog, he is in the back eating his dinner." Bond said nothing but relaxed his shoulders. Chris looked to Bond then over to Dave, "I've, or we have received no other information on the operation here. Father just told us to come here and get used to the area." Bond breathed out and contracted his shoulders back then grabbed his drink and looked into it examining the iced cubes and twirled it. "There are a lot of important people here in Vegas- not only the show people; stars need protection but important men that run the Valley… (he stopped and twirled his drink) well, certain people looking like they blend in."

Bond then broke his silence, "Protection," Dave nodded his head. "Right, I received a message from Vincent right before you came here. He said that he has arranged for certain people that you will learn from and he also stressed, really that a friend of his will is…soon living here and taking over the major operations. I suppose that means that both of you will be following him. Right now, this is what I do know." Bond instantly moved his head with a slight turn then became almost rigid in his seated position. Chris made a slight turn to him then regained his calm composure. "So, what are we supposed to do now?" Dave relaxed back in his chair holding his drink, and then laughed, "It's Vegas baby-have fun!"

After hearing this Chris laughed and took another sip of his drink as did Dave, Bond scrummed his head to the side and pushed forward his water. He then got up saying that he wasn't that hungry after all and returned to his room. They both watched him leave and go back to the house. Dave breathed out a heavy sigh. Chris knew that this was to open up the conversation with him. He put his arms forward then held them tight on his thighs taking a large breath in and breathed out while looking up the sky. There are just a lot of uncertainties right now, for both of us. A tall tanned thin figured young blonde approached them wearing a black and white flowered bikini sunglasses and a bamboo ribbon hat and high heels. Chris immediately thought no, for he was just married and that was it, he was married. He searched for words to say to Dave.

She smiled at him then placed her hands on Dave's shoulders while looking down at him. Dave then looked up to her and turned his face up to her, they both kissed. Seeing this relaxed Chris, he then smiled at the two of them. "Chris, I would like you to meet Barbie." Chris nodded his head to her then got up and moved back his chair for her to sit, which she did, he then left to go back in the house and wished them an as nice evening.

Now back in his room Chris looked out to the view, but instead of enjoying the night sky and the various colored lights all through the city, he closed the drapes then sat at the side end of the bed and grabbed his cell phone. He tried calling Jane. The line was busy, hearing the busy signal he tensed up his sitting body. Then he tried again hearing the same busy signal. Then after hearing the signal five times, he hung up the phone. He thought, why didn't it go to message? Was there something wrong? Maybe she was just having a good time with her friends, or maybe she was mad at him, he then thought why? Because he left her? He turned off the phone and then threw it to the carpeted floor. And then he just fell back on the bed. He moved up to support his head on the pillow, then opened and closed his eyes, breathed out loudly, then wiped his forehead then shook his head from side to side. What will tomorrow hold?

Bond paced back and forth in his darkroom; he closed the drapes but did not turn on a light. It was whether he wanted to blacken out the thought of no longer being in his home or losing the newfound seniority, or now suddenly thrust into being alone when it seemed that life was finally opening a new and wonderful chapter in his life. He collapsed his rigid body into a chair and sat there turning his head from side to side, and then moving the size of his pupils until he was certain that he could see in the darkened room. In one thrust he motioned forward out of the chair and turned his body to the left then right as like he was looking for an opposing force. There is just not enough room. He grabbed his jacket in one hand and with the other opened the door to the hallway.

Now in the hallway, he stopped and stepped back as Chris did the same. Chris looked straightforward to him and then replied, "You too?" Bond nodded his head, "Keys?" "I don't have them, do you?" They then went to Dave. Dave smiled then got up and went into the house and threw a set of keys, Chris caught them. Bond lifted his head to Dave, showing thanks. Dave nodded in return. "It's the gray one on the outside of the house."

Walking outside and turning in the direction of the parked car, they both stopped at it, and then looked to the other in question. Bond loudly replied, "This cannot be it. Use in that, this car…no." Chris had his head locked to only see the ground. He looked up only to throw the keys to Bond who caught them, then looked to Chris like you have to be kidding me. Chris already has his hand on the passenger door. Bond hesitantly unlocked it with the key and slowly sat in the driver's seat looking at everything in the car and then looked at his brother and raised his eyebrows. "This has to be the farthest stretch from a Ferrari possible, a

Toyota-Camry?" Chris replied, "It just keeps on getting better, doesn't it?" leaving the gated home, Bond said aloud, "This thing wouldn't have-on star, would it?" Chris looked only briefly at the dashboard, "No, have to use my phone. What places do we even go to? The only thing that I do know about Vegas is Caesars Palace." Bond quietly replied, "Well, it is a start." Dodging the cars and the pedestrians and waiting at a left turn light four times because the traffic was so backed up, they couldn't even go any further in the direction of the light. They both breathed a sigh of relief exiting the car in the parking garage of Caesar's Palace. After exiting the elevator to the main floor, then taking another hallway and turning past a food court, they wondered where the gambling even was another brief walk, and slot machines and tourists everywhere.

They commented to each other that they just were not in the mood to take part in this. They then walked an overhead walkway on the second floor and got over to the entrance to the flamingo hotel.

They took the stairs down to the street level then went inside to instant gambling. Ladies there gambling instantly turned their heads to Chris. He saw this then started walking in their direction; Bond grabbed his arm and pulled him away. He led them both further to the middle of the building, to the 21 tables. He nodded his head and they both sat at the same table just a seat separating the two of them with an older looking Hispanic man between them. A young handsome dealer named Jeff, from his name tag, welcomed them to the table and each put forth the money to buy chips. Jeff then dealt the cards out to the table.

After over an hour of playing, they each tipped the dealer then sat at a table in the food court which was to the left side of the gambling area. Chris held open his phone studying it like checking on texts. Bond sipped on the straw from his soda, and then in turn checked his texts. There was one from Chris saying that everything seemed to check out that they were safe. Bond texted back that he thought they should still leave but Chris texted show. Bond texted, Sitting Duck. Chris then texted to word to Bond, they both smiled and left.

Now in front of the Wynn, they exited the long stretch black limo and were instantly greeted by uniformed staff men. They were accompanied through the hotel and to the famed Sinatra steak house. There were two astute men dressed in a formal black suit standing at the entrance to this restaurant and they were informed by them that at this time it was reservation only. A simple head nod was given by one of the men who accompanied them there and they were let in and seated at a rear table. Chris noted as they walked past the bar, it was a small size to his taste 6 bars tools in front and it looked like 2 seats to the side, the bar had a mirrored back been liquor bottles were shelved.

The red cotton tablecloths adorned every table. White columns wherever they could be, it was formal. They were seated at a table for 6, where three gentlemen were already there and had drinks and appetizers in front of them. The larger older gentlemen in the middle, Bond thought from his looks, was in his late 60's and rotund physic and thick gray hair and large dark shaded eyeglasses. After handshakes and a brief introduction, he was the head of securities at the main financial institution in the city. From recent dealings, he found or thought that he was being followed and his computer, the private laptop had been hacked into twice.

Security even more than he already had was needed as his holdings were tied into the bank's mainframe where quite a few high-profile various holdings of important people and businesses were kept. A beautiful woman cocktail server came by the table to take drink orders. Mr. Garrison ordered a repeat on a Manhattan, Chris of course ordered his Martini and Bond a coke. The drinks were set on the table, Bond thought in only seconds after they ordered them. He then thought that this was probably from Mr. Garrison's stature in the city. More talk of questions being answered by him from Chris on basically everything. That had to do with his daily dealings. Bond said nothing during this scope of questioning, listening while keeping an eye on the dealings of the room.

They were only interrupted when the waiter came by to take their dinner orders. Before either Bond or Chris could get a word out while holding open their menus, Mr. Garrison blurted out that, the Veal Parmigiana was the only thing to get there. They both nodded their heads, Chris first to do so and ordered that. More conversation eluded until they were served and indeed the meal was fantastic as the service. Naturally more drinks were brought to them through the course of the meal.

Bond felt a bit queasy as the feeling of a roller-coaster. He excused himself to the restroom.

Inside the bathroom, he saw that he was alone. Still, he did a visual sweep of the room as something did just not feel right. He questioned the entire dilemma at that moment and momentarily longed for the comfort of home. He looked at his reflection in the bathroom mirror and then stopped his movement almost looking scared to see the questioning look that was looking back at him. He then deduced that he was going to have to change to fit into this new life whether he wanted to or not. He breathed out in giving up- then stiffened his back standing up straight then wiped his face on a bathroom towel. He took his hand and moved it over the side of his head with his fingers moving through each strand of hair on that side of his head. He then lunged to each side quickly straightened back up, breathed in, and then made a smile in the mirror and went back to the table.

In pulling his chair out he saw that the two men were enjoying a cup of espresso and he had a cup of coffee in front of his place at the table. He nodded to them and heard a Mr. Garrison laugh; a joke must have been told. He didn't hear it, nor did he want to. He fought the force to have the coffee. He didn't see it being poured and still questioned what was in his drink previous. He did take the cup firmly in his hand and took it off of the saucer occasionally moved it around the top of the tablecloth and even motioned it up to his mouth, but he never took a drink from it. He just sat there and listened until goodbyes were exchanged, and they all walked out of the restaurant.

Bond walked to the side of Chris holding his failing body. He made as quickly, yet as safe as he could to the front where the same black limo was there. Bond opened the back door and helped Chris into it, then faster than you could see him move he entered on the other side of it and tapped for the driver to leave.

Once on the freeway, he called his dad and told him about what happened. The father and Vincent heard the news from Bond as he put the phone on loudspeaker, he said to be very careful and put things on hold for a time and stay at the new residence, and to meet Jonathan at the airport.

Jonathan boarded a private jet, before stepping onto the plane he turned his head and looked back taking inventory, watching for anything then in the calmest manner he tilted up his head and went aboard. Just ten minutes later the plane was air bound. He quietly slept for most of the flight then was awakened by a small bit of turbulence over the skies of California. He straightens up his body in the seat and looked around the plane. He heard the pilot say that it would only be a short time until landing.

Now parked on the Vegas runway, he waited until the guards came to open the plane and lift the stairs for his departure. He asked the main guard at the stairs if all was safe, and a swipe made. The guard shook his head confirming that everything was safe. Jonathan then calmly and sternly deboarded then entered the special entrance on the side of the main airport. Bond was waiting for him in the first room he entered. Each made a head nod to the other and them, but on protecting headgear, the wording of the Corona virus. His was a safety issue that at the moment paid off.

Now both inside the Camry, while buckling his seat belt Jonathan remarked to Bond, "Did you seriously lose everything that you had in a poker game, and had to leave with this?" Bond looked at him before stepping on the gas to leave him remarked back, "Something like that." Parked in front of Dave's estate Jonathan got out and automatically went to the front door. He made a quick "Hello" to Dave then nodded his head and went to Chris's bedroom. He saw that Chris was lying on his side hunched over holding his stomach looking queasy. He sat at the side of the bed and took his pulse. Chris looked up wide-eyed and frightened, Jonathan instantly knew what was wrong and he sprinted up from the bed leaving room for Chris to get to the bathroom. The sound of him belching was heard through the room and open door where Bond stood.

Jonathan calmly looked to Bond then placed his hand on his shoulder and led him back to the hallway. "There is nothing more wrong with your brother than a hangover. By mid-afternoon tomorrow, he'll be better. In need of clean clothes, but he'll be better."

Both of them, Bond and Jonathan, are now sitting in the living room and commencing conversation. Bond told Jonathan everything about the meeting the night before. Jonathan waved his hand to Bond. Bond leaned back and stopped his speech, then gave a rather evil smirk in response. Jonathan waited a moment before starting his speech. "This was, the whole night was a set-up. Do you know anything about him…Mr. Garrison? Have you ever looked into the files on the financial markets here in Vegas?" Bond recoiled his body further back in the chair. "That or this is all the answer that I need. You, you and your brother are like two bulls running into the pit with no knowledge of the situation. How many matadors are there? Are there people in the audience with guns? Remember back to spy school 101, do not go in a situation half-cocked."

Bond could do nothing but sink further into the chair and waited almost as to be forgiven. He swallowed hard looking as though he swallowed a cup of tea that was too hot and then lifted back his body-waiting for any other verbiage from Jonathan. Dave made a brief appearance before heading out the front door. Bond instantly stood up and welcomed Dave to Jonathan.

Handshakes and smiles were exchanged then Dave threw up his car keys, caught them then headed out the door. He seems nice. Bond moved his head to air then twisted it around relieving tension then replied, "he is."

Jonathan then explained to Bond that he had a lot of pressing matters to attain to. He did turn on the television while in the motion of leaving. In hearing the voice from the local news, he stopped instantly in his motion, froze then reacted as he had just seen a ghost. On the screen was the commentator than a quick flash to the governor of the state- Steve Sisolak. The state was on immediate lockdown from the Corona virus. All business' schools, department stores, churches, especially casinos, are now closed. Stay at home, orders are now instantly enforced.

Jonathan moved his quiet lifeless body sinking into the chair. Bond looked up not even remember seeing him leave the area of the front door, and then breathed out heavily. Jonathan moved his hand to his forehead lifted it off while breathing out. A quick noise was heard- both instantly moved their heads to the side of the room. Chris appeared still a bit unsteady in his stance, but he stood there with both of their attentions on him. "What are we going to do now?" Bond was surprised that he already was aware of this latest news, but then he thought- this is his brother- a highly trained spy.

Both Bond and Jonathan opened their mouths to speak out on the answer to this question though no words were heard. Chris turned his body leaving the room then he moved his head to the side view of them and replied, "We have to check out." Bond replied questioning, "But we aren't even there." Chris retorted from down the hall. "Exactly, that is the problem." Bond lifted his head after taking seconds to think of this, then got up and went to the hallway to his room and get ready to "check out."

Now both men were ready to leave had stopped to meet with Jonathan before leaving. Jonathan smiled at them then quickly asked them, "Have either of you called your father to make sure that he is alright?" In not receiving an instant response, he took that as a no. He stepped back from him holding his cell phone and proceeding to dial, "I'll do it. You two just go and go now!"

Bond drove as he was better acquainted with the road directions. Chris moved uncomfortably in his seat, whether it was because he wasn't the driver or because he was still feeling some of the hangover, or maybe because he hadn't heard from his wife. Exiting off of the freeway, Bond looked to Chris and replied to him, "All three bases are loaded, aren't they?" Chris knew what Bond meant and at first thought how did he know what he was thinking, but then thought of the utter closeness of the two of them. He breathed in then swallowed and replied, "Yes."

Without a moment's hesitation Bond parked in the garage of the hotel then they went to their rooms and opened the doors, at the same time both did a quick sweep, then opened their bags and went through them looking especially for any "bugs". They reached the doors at the same time, then went down the elevator to the checkout line which was more than long and noisy with guests crying in fear of this new epidemic that was plaguing the world, the country, and there, right there on home turf. It felt like living through a science fiction movie, the spine trembled in the desperation of the unknown contagion.

After never-ending minutes, they checked out to the same name that they checked in, they were quiet being careful not to say or feel the wrong thing. Walking to the side hall to the parking garage they were escorted to the side of the front drive-up entrance. Panic overwhelmed Bond then he quickly looked to his brother's reaction and saw no fear. He wondered was everything alright or was this part of the plan? He then noted the family crest on the guard's gold bracelet to his right side. The backside door of a black limo was opened by one of the guards, Chris as usual was the first inside, and then Bond, the door was instantly closed by one of the guards. The vehicle was then in motion leaving the parking lot. Chris made no affirmation and remained quiet. Bond was still an incomplete question and a slight bit of fear.

At the red stoplight to the freeway entrance, the window was opened to see and speak to the driver. It was Jonathan. "I presume everything went alright at checkout." Bond relaxed his body sinking into the backseat and thought, how did he know, but he didn't want to show any vulnerability to the situation and remained quiet. As soon as we get back, there are a lot of things that we have to go over. The light changed green and the pressure and movement of the motion were felt. The window then closed. Chris closed his eyes, Bond saw this then noticed his brother's left hand slightly shake and only the three fingers on it moved; the middle finger to the pinky, bending back and forth repeatedly - he had this nervous trait ever since childhood. Bond knew that Chris was thinking and worried about his wife, Jane.

Bond took his open hand to his mouth and breathed out, then held his breath as he was very nervous about it or her too. He thought he heard Jonathan say that he was going to look into its bit being that he picked him up at the hotel, plans had changed. On what seemed the long drive back to Dave's home both of them had fallen asleep. Before parking, Jonathan opened the window seeing this and was surprised by this, but then in a way glad. "Okay boys were now back in the land of Oz," he stepped out of the car, and then the side door where Bond sat was opened. As he turned to view - he noted that Chris was already standing behind him wiping the sleepiness off of his face.

Inside the living room seated at the dining table at the right side of the room, there was a silver metal pot of espresso and espresso cups at the front of each one of them. Chris nodded his head to Jonathan while he placed a spoonful of sugar in his cup then held it, cradling it and looked at it almost as if though waiting for an answer from it. His tightness showed over his relaxed composure. Bond sat, breathed out then ran his opened hands down his thighs, then reached up to his coffee and took a sip. Seeing this other two did the same.

Jonathan then took over the moment. "Alright, we are on a puzzle board." He loved his view across the round table looking directly opposite to Chris and noticed that he did not have his facial attention to his eye view. He clanked a spoon on the table to capture his attention. He nodded his head then began his speech. He at first breathed out then bit his lips which prompted Chris to full attention fearing what was going to be said. Bond in turn gave his full attention.

"Jane and Lauren have moved from their California home and are no longer in California." Chris moved his head over the table closer to the direction of Jonathan. The following seconds were pure silence, as fear circled the air of the room in Chris's mind. Jonathan instantly picked up on this. Bond just sat there entranced. "She is safe, she is…,"Jonathan paused to swallow. Chris moved closer to him, his upper body now on the table.

"She is with your father in Hawaii." Once Chris heard this, he breathed out a long sigh, then showed an instant relief over his face than the body. Bond relaxed his tightened mood, and then took a sip of the coffee and Chris did as well waiting to hear more from Jonathan. Jonathan first sensed this then saw it.

Bond then asked him how his father was. Chris quickly quipped, "Jane? Lauren?" he took a brief swallow of coffee then started in verse. "Jane is fine and Lauren also, it is Vincent." Chris almost dropped his cup. Jonathan quickly proceeded back to the verse. "Your father has had a heart tremor and is now in the hospital. He has asked that Bond goes to him and go to him now." Chris extorted, "him" looking furiously to his brother. "Why him, and not me? My wife and daughter are there, it should be me!" Bond gave a side brief glaring view to his brother then looked to Jonathan for an answer. "Look, I do not want any trouble from either one of you. I am just relaying what your father said to me. And he DID say that Bond knew." Bond knew full well of what this meant, as Vincent did sit him in the office and had the conversation about him taking over the family reins. Chris still showed anger and contempt over his frazzled body.

Bond got up from the chair then made an inquisitive look to Jonathan, then said, "I better get ready to leave now. Did you, have you made the plane reservation for me?" Jonathan peered to Chris as he moved in contempt and was almost spitting in anger as he fought with himself to stay in the chair. It was quite evident that if he did get up a boxing match would be front in center of the room. Jonathan took a piece of paper then handed it to Bond. He took it walking away not even looking at it. Bond now out of view, Chris looked to Jonathan who was not showing any emotion and again quipped to him, "Why him?" he then got up and twirled his body in anger, then looked for a way to go left unmoved in his path. Jonathan threw him a set of car keys. "Take a drive and cool off, but be careful. Oh, and take my car, it is the deep blue Bentley, Continental GT."

Chris raised his eyebrows as he knew about the car that Jonathan spoke of, and was more than impressed, a complete 180 from the Toyota. Chris held open the hand containing the keys and looked at them twice and was then awestricken, Jonathan sensed this and got up from the table. He took three steps to the side then paused at the still unmoved man and said,

"You're welcome." Before he could even leave the room, his cell phone went off. Jonathan looked at Chris and then nodded his head to him. He then left the room. Chris slowly took the phone and answered the call. In just hearing the voice of what it was, he quickly made it to a chair and sank into it.

He breathed out listening to his wife's voice. He showed a brief second of happiness then deleted his fear of listening to what she was going to say to him. "Oh, I am okay, how are you doing?" he listened transfixed in the thought that she hadn't been mentioned Vincent yet. She was already four or five sentences in her speech to him, and he didn't hear "I miss you" or when will we see each other. In every following word that he did hear that she spoke to him, none were of any importance to him; he literally felt his heart sinking as his body plunged deeper into the chair.

"So, how long are you going to stay there, and how is Lauren? My daughter?" A brief pause as he moved his feet out to side then brought them back together. "Oh, is she getting into school there? No, that sounds good." He moved his head briefly to each side then asked her when she was going to come and see him. Hearing her response, he almost fell out of the chair. "You do not like southern CA, but I am in…," he stopped his speech. Then he again listened to her. "Yeah, a yes, I guess that he does need you there, how is he?" he again listened. "You haven't seen him yet today, well is this good news or bad?" he quickly got his sinking body up from the chair. "You are breaking up, I can hardly hear you, are you okay? Do I need to be there, are you alright?" At that moment Chris looked like he could just jump to where she was to save her. "What? What? I can hardly hear you." He heard a barely audible response back to him, "You have to go." "Goodbye, Jane, I love you." He waited and heard nothing, no response, nothing, the lines just went dead.

He walked two feet ahead, then turned and looked to the front door, then turned and looked out of the window. On the other side of him, he saw that Jonathan was still there. He looked at him and smiled, "I guess I will take that drive after all." Jonathan nodded his head showing every meaning in that nod. He started down the hallway to his room to change his clothes, but then thought of his brother's room directly across from his and at that moment he just did not want to see him.

He more than admired the blue Bentley before getting into it. Now inside, he adjusted the mirror and the seat. In just turning the key and starting the engine, he felt like he was listening to a happy cat purr. Oh, the sound was rhythmical and relaxing he could feel his body release. There was so much pleasure in feeling himself in control.

Pressing on the accelerator he couldn't hear a noise from the car. He only stopped long enough for the electric gate to open then curved around the next turn and brought his sunglasses from the top of his head back down to the temple of his nose and smiled even wider. Down the few side streets to the main road where he felt more at ease then followed the road signs to the freeway. He then took the exit to take him to Caesars Palace. Now on the seemingly barren Vegas Strip Street, he could not believe the emptiness and desperation that he felt when seeing this. "This looks and feels like something out of a science fiction movie…. the only question is: when is the monster, space alien or bad guy show up?" Just after he finished this last word, he reminded himself of his job and that being there was not a vacation. There was no place open to going. "This has to be the worst pandemic known to mankind."

He viewed the empty fountains in front of the Bellagio and the barren streets. Every now and then a taxi would go by in the other direction. "This is not what I am looking for. How could mankind allow this to happen?" he then saw three people walking down the street, they all had masks on. "Well, it is not Halloween, but there is certainly a fear of it, a monster that we cannot presently kill." He took the next exit out of there. Now back on the freeway, it was almost barren also. He momentarily hummed the theme from a monster movie. And then tried to laugh, but he couldn't. He had driven down many streets from the exit; peaceful trees lined each side of the street. It was most welcoming. He then slowed up though no other cars were in front of him or behind him. A young woman was standing to the side of her SUV on the side of the road and the hood was up. He immediately thought, trouble both possibly for her but definitely for him. He fought his gut instinct to just drive by and not notice but manliness overshadowed that.

He pulled off the side of the road and parked behind her. She smiled at him, but then he could tell that she straightened up her stance. He momentarily stopped his pace toward her and then sprang into dialogue. She instantly lost her smile and expressed a look of worry. She moved her head like giving him the leeway to come forward and help her. "Listen, Miss, I know that you do not know who I am and I can understand your resistance- but I assure you that I am just offering my help. I do know just a little about cars." After he finished this last sentence, he defiantly had to hold a laugh back.

She nodded her head and then walked to the open hood of her car he followed. He proceeded to check her fluids, and everything was okay. He then asked her to start it, and then get out as he checked the control panel of the driver's view. "There is just one more thing that I need to check." He got out and went back to the front of the engine. "You need to start the car while I check something." With hesitancy and fear on her face, she did this. She saw him pull something out of the engine, then put it back in and take it out again and he viewed this. While he was in the act of doing this, a police car pulled up to the side of them. She instantly showed a look of panic. The 40ish tall brown wavy-haired white policeman wearing dark glasses immediately went to the open car engine.

The policeman now standing in front of them asked them what the problem was. She started a dialogue and stumbled on the words. Chris jumped into the conversation. "We know about the need to be sheltered so to say and we were both leaving to go home to make sure that our parents are okay. I live with them as I have just gone through a divorce. This is, she is my sister…And we were just going together, and this happened to her car, good thing that I was behind her." "Miss, I am going to need to see your driver's license." She panicked but Chris motioned shush to her. They all turned their heads hearing the sound of a vehicle approaching. It was an AAA truck. "I did call them to help." The officer then proceeded into speech. "But, you're…brother," he stopped to lower his dark glasses looking at Chris.

Then he was interrupted by his pager going off calling him to an emergency. He started walking away. And while leaving, he remarked again, "It is a good thing that you called her help." Chris felt a pang from that remark. He asked her again if she would like him to stay until she felt comfortable with everything. He saw her hesitancy in replying to him, so he waited to explain everything to the repairman and stayed to watch him charge the vehicle. Her car now was in service, and Chris asked her she had a good repair shop to go to.

She didn't answer him. He waved goodbye while she was still standing at the door of her car.

He drove down many further streets having no idea where he was, but he really didn't notice anything that he drove by anyway. He turned his head to see a golf course; its beauty looked rather out of place compared to what the area surrounding it. Only then did he come back to his senses at the seriousness of the present situation and of how, he wasn't in Hawaii, home- to see his father or for that matter his wife. He then thought of their phone conversation and of how he thought that she almost acted callous to him, but why? Was there someone else? And Bond is going there or even is there now.

He checked road directions, and then turning to go back to what was now home base, he remarked, "But he is my brother." He started to speed once on the freeway and then thought of the snide police officer from earlier and instantly lowered his speed. "What am I doing here?" he took the next exit, he knew that it wasn't the one he needed to get to the base, but he had so much angered frustration running through his veins and he thought this needed picking up. Almost as if he knew it would be there, just 4 blocks from the exit to the right was a sporting goods shop. He parked, and then went in to find what he wanted, then returned to the parking lot with a large cardboard box.

He stopped to look at the box then the circumference of the inside of the car, he only stopped long enough to scratch his head, then put all the seats down except for the drivers and crammed it inside the car. Instead of feeling the happiness of the accomplishment he lifted up his arms with closed fists, then stepped back and walked to the back of the building. Hearing a voice stopped him, then he opened his eyes and looked to a large metal dumpster that he would have run into if the "voice" hadn't stopped him.

He lowered his head then stepped forward, closed his eyes, and focused on the man who said this. "Matt?" he stepped closer. The man then looked at Chris, turned his head, and then stopped looking like he just figured out a Rubik's cube. They both walked to each other and hugged briefly then stepped back. Laughter filled the air and then the conversation started. "My God, I haven't seen you since." Chris interrupted him, "we're not that old."

Matt smiled, then said, "Karate class." "Yeah, I remember, but that was in Hawaii, what are you doing here?" he walked over to a wooden bench in the back of the building; Chris followed and sat down beside him.

"Gosh, it has been so long. I got married and she wanted to go to the Mainland, we moved around a bit then finally settled here in Vegas and now I manage this sports shop. No kids, we tried it just hasn't worked. What about you?" Chris then gave him a brief rundown of his life, a few things not mentioned, and he finished by saying that he came here to start a new life also. Matt briefly walked back inside the building and Chris did nothing more than relax and shield his eyes from the sun's glare then scooted down the bench a little, where it no longer shined in his eyes. Matt came back from the building holding a six-pack of Miller lite. He took two off the holder and handed one to Chris. Chris nodded in appreciation. He held the can back then opened it. Matt then asked him if there was something wrong. He shook his head no, and then proceeded to drink.

They rambled on in laughter for nearly an hour. Then Matt got up and said that he needed to get home to the misses. He then said to Chris, "It is a miracle that no one has caught you yet." Getting up and then standing his stance, "Well, you know me." They both laughed and Chris threw the can inside the dumpster, then left, this time to return to base and assemble the punching bag.

Now in Hawaii, Bond got off the plane. He was more than thankful for the empty seats around him that he was sure his father or someone made it happen this way. He picked up his bag from the luggage collection then started to walk to the parking lot, then stopped and let out a deep sigh; his car was not there waiting for him as usual. He slowed his steps knowing the only option was for a cab. He shook his head and then started to one and was caught with a foreign hand to his chest. He almost jumped. But then saw it was an airport guard telling him of the line for cabs and it was behind him. He smiled then nodded and went to the back of the line. He thought, what else could happen? He was happily surprised that the line moved very quickly. Once seated inside after the driver checked to make sure that he did fasten his seat belt. The driver started a conversation about everything and anything.

When he was asked questions from the driver he sat quietly and looked out the side window. He knew that he shouldn't take it to the estate, but what was his other option, his brother wasn't there to pick him up and his dad was not in commission. Then he noticed of the neighborhood and the drive and asked the cab to let him out at the diner where he saw the woman that he met at her home when he had car trouble.

Opening the door to get inside, he stumbled on himself, then dropped his bad and fought with the door, then finally got a hold of the gripping of the bead then knocked his fist on the door. Excruciating pain traveled down his shoulder to his hand and he wanted to yell in pain, but he took two deep swallows and then breathed out heavily in attempts to hide it. Laurie was wiping tables in the empty restaurant, and then hearing the noise she was about to say aloud, "We're closed," and then seeing her audience, she raised her head then folded her arms with the folded cloth and smiled to him. Hearing no words from the now composed Bond, she started her speech to him. "I knew that you would be back, I do make good coffee." They both laughed and then he tried in words that just seemed to end half-way through each sentence. She walked to the back kitchen, placed the towel in the hamper, closed the lid and then locked the back door and grabbed her bags proceeding to leave out the front door which Bond arrived through.

She held open the door for him to leave, he scrambled out and followed her around to the side of the building to her car and got in. She could tell of his dilemma but made no questions regarding the matter. This captivated Bond- he thought and hoped that she would be the "right" woman for him.

And truly right now, he needed somebody or something.

In following his directions, she stopped at the gates to the estate. She looked up to them then turned her head twice looking for him, "You are a spy...I mean this?" Bond bit his lip not wanting to go through any family business at that moment. After the gate opened, she slowly drove in. She stopped as the dogs came out running and barking. She parked and he got out, again stumbling on his words to thank her. She sensed him, and the stillness of his quietness of speaking no response to her made her feel the uneasiness of the moment. Then in the next brief she composed herself saying that she had to get home and to lady and she'd take a rain check on the Martini. Bond smiles and lets out a slight laugh feeling warmth in his heart. She rose up her head, then nodded to him and left the estate.

Inside the house, after placing his bags in his room he opened the door to the office only to be greeted by the empty chair behind the desk. He froze his body to the scene, then shook his head from side to side and swallowed, then stood there in silence for the brief moment. He went to the kitchen, opened the refrigerator, and grabbed a bottle of beer. Then he stopped in motion to twist off the cap and he just looked at the bottle. "I can't do this, and I mean this in more ways than one…but I have to, I have no other choice." He dropped his arms still holding the bottle firmly in his hand, and then put it back in the refrigerator, then took out a can of Dr. Pepper instead. He walked to the window and looked out to the ocean while popping it open, then took one swig followed by another then another until the can was empty.

He went back to his room and changed his clothes, used the bathroom then walked out back to the kitchen; he opened the drawer, took out the keys to the SUV and left the house. He's now driving into the lot of the hospital and honestly didn't even remember getting there. Walking to the doors of the hospital, he noticed a line of people then saw that he had to get in this line. He thought of the inspection that you go through before boarding a plane; he then quickly realized that they were checking those waiting to enter for fever and then giving them face masks to put on before going in the building. He then immediately knew it was because of the Corona virus pandemic. He was happy to see this and thought of the terrible dreaded disease plaguing the world, but he had to see and get to his father.

Once at the Critical Care Unit of the hospital, he had to sign papers, and then waited in a small room. There were two chair banks opposite each other, and a TV mounted on the middle wall. He sat down and there were two other persons, both elderly white females with their heads down in what looked like a prayer. Not wanting to know of their grief, he looked away and saw the only option besides looking at the door was the television. He looked up then felt the weight of his enormous grief and responsibility, he looked up at the voices coming from the tube. After just a minute into watching it, he saw it was the older Mac Gyver series with Richard Dean Anderson, he remembered in his early years that he did watch and enjoy this show. It most definitely helped pass time.

He drew his own conclusion to the outcome of the story and then he heard his name called. He started up from the seat then fell back down into it, then in a firmer manner raised his body up from the chair and followed the female nurse down the hallway. She placed another mask over the mask that he was wearing then gloves over his hands. As he walked inside the room seeing his father hooked up to various machines and the pinging sounds filling the otherwise silent air, he then smelled the utter scent of a medical facility, he thought, "Am I seeing death? I don't want to." He took a moment to stand to the side of the metal raised bed, and really looked to his father. His eyes were closed. And he then wondered, how his father would even know that he was there?

His eyes swelled with tears, he closed them and slowly, ever so slowly reopened them. He then felt there was a missing puzzle piece that he needs to find to change this and change it now. He mouthed words, though no sound came out, he then blinked again and reached down to his father's hand and held it. In a quiet trembling voice, he whispered, "Dad." Only five seconds passed and he felt a tight squeeze to his on hand. "He's, he is alive, and he is okay." The nurse in the room then explained to him that the body often goes through this, and it probably is just his body moving. Bond then thought no, my father knows that I am here, I am here, here. Vincent then opened his eyes. Bond became elated with joy. Vincent then opened and closed his eyes again and said aloud, "Bond, I know that you are here."

The nurse then saw this, wrote something down in the chart, and left the room. Only a minute passed and a doctor returned to the room and Bond was motioned out. He waited in the waiting room for what seemed like hours and was then called back and was told that they didn't expect this to happen and that Vincent with the age and ailing health, they started to explain an option to Bond. Once he heard them say nursing home, he yelled out, "No. My father's wishes are to return home and we will provide care."

This was against what he was told, but then the next moment Bond was on his phone making the necessary arrangements for Vincent's return.

# Chapter 3

THE GATE TO the estate opened, Bond drove in and was followed by an ambulance carting his father. Parked in the front portico of the house, Bond instantly unlocked the front door, then ran to the ambulance and gave the driver directions on what to do next. Vincent very carefully was taken out of the back and wheeled to the front door. Once there he was placed in a wheelchair. Bond was given further instructions on the care of his dad. Bond noticed a car parked to the side of the house in the direction of the garage. An older middle-age woman exited her car and went to talk to Bond. She was the caretaker that Bond sent to make sure that his dad got the proper care. She was a nurse that specialized in geriatrics. He then said some more words to the driver before it left the estate.

Bond ran in the house only stopping to close the front door. The woman nurse, whose name was Maggie, then asked Bond the direction of his father's bedroom. Bond first pointed then thought better of it and ran showing her the way there. He only stopped at the door of the room to open it, and then his dad was rolled to his bed. Bond helped Maggie get Vincent in his bed and settled. Bond only stopped long enough to lift his head up, gather a much-needed breath of air and took a very brief pause before laying his hand ever so gently on his father's hand. He felt no squeeze or motion from his dad. The nurse noticed this and explained how he must be very tired, and he needed to rest after the long ordeal of the trip there.

Bond nodded his head and then left the room. The nurse stayed in the room on a chair beside the bed.

He then retreated to his room-changed into a tee shirt and sweat pants. Looking in the mirror, he made a look of judgment, then closed his eyes and splashed his face with cold water then returned to the living room. He more than hoped that the cook had been there that day and left something for or was cooking dinner. He didn't go to check and see, he was contemplating in his mind on whether to have a drink or not. He stood there and looked at the tide pull back and then fall to the shore motion after motion. It was relaxing at that moment, seeing, and getting the feeling that everything was in motion.

He then went to the liquor cart on the left side of the room. He stood over the tray of liquor bottles; some full, some only half- full then circles his open hand over the bottles. He then took back his hand in one motion and said aloud to himself, "for the past 6 years, I have only drunk wine at dinner. I am in recovery, and I am no longer an alcoholic." He stepped back almost jumping from it. Then he took hold of the bottle of Vodka and poured it to the utter top of a glass. He picked it up balancing it so easily; he brought to his mouth, and then put his upper lip over the rim of the glass.

He walked to the couch and sat down with a drink in hand. He watched as the liquid inside the glass swirled. He raised his hand bending them, then leaned back sitting straight up on the couch. He breathed in then raised his head, then his chin went down to his neck very tightly raising his shoulders in the same tight fashion. He then bent his elbows with hands on his lap and drew in another breath, then stood up and actually backed away from the couch while looking at the glass on the table. Before he left the room, he looked again back to the table and the full glass, "I won, you didn't."

In the kitchen he smelled a relaxing smell, then the cook was just packing up to leave for the evening, explaining that her husband was sick and she wanted to get back home to him. In a very needy voice, she asked if she could leave early. Bond showed concern and simply nodded his head. After he heard the side door close as she left, he pulled his hand to his mouth then wiped his lips, opened his mouth, and let out a breath.

He opened the oven door and the enticing smell of food again filled the air-it was calming.

With oven mitts he pulled out the covered casserole and placed it on the counter, lifting the lid he saw it was fettuccine Alfredo, an Italian classic. He played himself, then took it to the dining room then sat down and took a bite. His eyes closed as he truly enjoyed it. He then thought of his dad and the nurse. He pulled back in the chair then grabbed one more bite before going to his father. Standing by the door partially open, he explained to Maggie of the food. She told him that it was too early for his dad to eat and she was fine. He felt relief through guilt still followed him as he went back to the table. The only pause that he made in the course of eating this was when he went to the kitchen and came back with a glass of ice and a bottle of Pellegrino to finish this blessed meal.

After cleaning up in the kitchen Bond goes to check on his dad. The lights in the room have been dimmed, giving the room a more peaceful feeling. Bond saw and heard a slight snore from his dad. Maggie lifted her head from a book and gave a smile to Bond. He tipped his head and smiled at her then left. In his mind, he thought one less thing to worry about. He went inside his room, and then unpacked his bags, straightened up the bed then sat diagonally at the end of it. "No time to mourn about anything," he then called his brother's burner phone. He waited patiently counting every ring. There was no answer. He then thought, is he in trouble? Or was he doing this deliberately? He spread his legs, then ran his hands down his thighs then retracted his head and neck to the ceiling.

"Well, Jonathan is there." He walked out to the veranda and noticed the light welcome breeze to this 76-degree evening - he liked this, but didn't smile and showed no emotion to anything. Before taking a visual sweep of the area, he said aloud, "Laurie." He then went to the beach and started his run. After four quick sprints back and forth on the coastline, he stopped breathing out heavily and bent over. Jane came up and stood beside him. He made no notice of her. She was a bit taken aback by this then tapped his back. He turned into a fast motion spy and grabbed her tightly, pressing in; she screamed out, "It's me, Jane!" he instantly let loose then retracted back from her.

She made a look of concern to his distance from her. "It's good to see you, Bond." He took two more steps further from her, "likewise, I haven't heard from Chris, have you?"

Anger came over her face, she instantly lost all happiness that she expressed seeing Bond. "Why?" She momentarily pouted, then turned away from him and quickly walked back to the house. He watched her leave not knowing what to think then said aloud another puzzle piece that doesn't fit.

# Chapter 4

J ONATHAN FINISHED UNPACKING and arranging things at his new condo in Vegas, it's in a quiet gated community. At the kitchen table, he made himself a cup of tea and watched it for a moment, then poured a cup and took a long soothing sip. Just as he finished his second sip the doorbell rang. He breathed out exasperated, then said aloud, "Is it girl scouts selling cookies?" he pulled a handgun out of a kitchen drawer and placed it in his back pocket. It turned out to be an older retired couple that lived across the street from him in the next building. They introduced themselves and all he could think of was about how his tea was getting cold and of how much he wanted to get rid of them. He finally interjected on the old woman's speech and thanked them but told them he had a phone call to get back to. He nodded, said thank you then closed the door on them. Standing behind the closed door, he could hear old woman's speech, and knew that he did not want to hear it. He went back to his tea. After finishing a cup then starting on the second cup the doorbell rang again. It was the building manager asking if everything was alright. He smiled at him then said it was and closed the door again returning to his welcoming tea.

Back at the table, he took a sip, then made a fowl expression and put it down saying aloud, "It's cold." He leaned back in the chair and then made a questioning look. "Do I want more and change it or go for a beer?" he took the cup to the sink then opened the refrigerator. He grabbed a cold bottle of beer and heard the doorbell. He placed it back in the refrigerator, then collapsed his body before going to the door. In that moment of feeling utter defeat and wanting to end this cycle, he opened the front door wide without even checking who was there.

Before even noticing the three men dressed in movers' uniforms, he noticed the large moving truck parked on the street in front of his dwelling. He then lowered his head to the faces of these men. He thought it odd that they were not the same faces of the men that moved him there. right as he opened his mouth to question them, a rag was crammed in his mouth, then he was gut-punched then a heavy cloth was placed over his face. He fought, but in each movement he became weaker. The back lift of the van was rolled up, then his body was put inside. One man secured it with two padlocks before it drove away.

# Chapter 5

DRIVING- CHRIS MISSED the correct exit to get back to base. He didn't notice it until it was too late. He took the next exit thinking that he could turn around there and get back the other way. To his surprise, there was no entrance in the direction that he needed to go. He silently cussed about it, still moving his lips to what he meant to say out loud. He took the next turn that he could to the right thinking that he'd make a U-turn there and try to get back somehow. At just a few feet down the road, a cement separation was between the lanes, making it impossible to do this. With no other option, he continued down this business road.

The street came to a dead-end at a storage facility. A large moving truck was parked on the side front of it. The gates to this facility were locked. As he slowed at the end of the street seeing no other option to make a U-turn there, he stopped, first unsure of what the moving truck was going to do as it had it is motor running, as he looked to it. The driver instantly looked to his right and the man in the passenger seat looked to his right. Chris had been a spy long enough to know that something was up here. He thought he can't make himself a mark, so in the same slow fashion he did turn and passed to the side of it very carefully - as he did this, he viewed the license plate and instantly memorized it.

He went down to the end of where the division started, then turned right and stopped at the side of that street parking to the side of a private condominium village, it was now residential. He waited for close to twenty minutes and did not see the truck come back from where it was parked with its motor running. He then decided that his only option was to get back on the freeway. He then thought maybe paranoia, there was just something odd about it.

Back to home base- Dave's place. He was assembling the punching bag at the backside of the garage. Dave came around wearing a loose white tee shirt and Bermuda shorts showing off his tan. He looked to Chris, who was in the process of finishing putting together the punching bag on its stand. Dave paused about to open his mouth to say something but waiting for Chris to lead the conversation since he knew that Chris had spotted him. Dave took the moment and started a dialogue, "Are you taking up a new hobby, there?" Chris just huffed in response. Dave waited for another minute-only to hear silence then seeing the maddened look expressed from Chris, he left.

A marked security vehicle approached the storage facility, the moving van was still parked there with a nod exchanged by each driver. There were no cars or people in sight. The security car punched the code to get into the facility, and then the driver ran out of the car and unlocked the metal box next to the front office. Then he punched a code turning off the alarm. He got back in the car then drove around to the side of the front building out of view from the street. The van drove in and then took the first right it could be the size of the van. The second building around the side of that entrance it stopped at the driver of the security car then unlocked a truck-size metal roll top entrance. The van backed in.

Smaller storage units inside, then had its opening rolled up- boxes were placed inside, then the moving shackled body of Jonathan was pushed out of the truck and he fell. Two men picked him up and carried him to an open unit, his body fell almost weightless to the ground and then he was pushed further in. A medium-framed white man dressed very nicely, then emerged and watched this. "Come on men, let's show some compassion." He throws in a plastic water bottle then loudly laughed as the storage unit was closed with Jonathan inside.

# Chapter 6

**B**OND WENT BACK to the house. He took a trip to the kitchen to see that it was empty, at that point he greatly missed his family.

After taking a bottle of water in silence, he hummed to himself then proceeded to the office. He sat back in the chair of the desk, moved his body around, but it was almost like he could not find a place there. "I have no choice. I…have to do it." He turned on the computer then entered his father's code to read all the messages.

The first few were just of his father's friends making and exchanging small talk. "Nothing of any importance." He let out a deep sigh, and then scrolled down the messages. He raised his eyes then sat up straight in the chair seeing a message from Jonathan, and it was a message from that day yet. He instantly went to it.

"There is a shell company here in Vegas, have been doing some investigation to it. It seems a large moving company just went bankrupt a month ago, right now with this present pandemic; people are not paying attention to businesses that have gone under. Trading is being transported by them. I almost found them. I have a realistic lead; I will pursue tomorrow. You take care" - V. J.

I knew it; he clenched his fists then leaned back in the chair-wheeled it back then took a light breath and let out a deep breath of relief. He then dialed Jonathan's number on his cell phone…no answer. "What is it with

Vegas, no one answers their phones." He got up then went to his room ready to pack his bag to go there, then quickly realized with his father's condition and the way things presently were, he couldn't… he stopped in motion then clenched his arm and moved it up and down, then did a 180 with his body and started punching at the air. "This is when I normally go to dad, for an answer, but right now, I am a dad. Think, think." He went back to the office then sat down moving from side to side then again took out his phone and dialed Chris. "I really need to talk to you right now, please answer." He got a busy signal. He smiled hearing this. "I'll try back in a few minutes. I had better go through all of these other messages." He took a sip of water then engrossed himself in this.

Chris had the punching bag put together on its stand, sweat poured from his head, he moved the back of his hand wiping it. He flew his arm up to the bag, it rocked. He calmly stepped back from it and gave it a slight ponder. After that he went through, to put it together there was definitely something wrong on why he wasn't using it. He took two more steps back to the side to be in the shade then took his cell phone from his pocket and dialed Jane's number. It rang a total of seven times and no option to leave a message. "What is wrong with her?" he hung up and then saw a message that his brother Bond had called. He first smiled, then stood back and grimaced. He scratched the side of his face, then looked out to the valley then the phone and closed his eyes. "Him, she is with him."

Chris stepped back breathed out into rhythm counting to ten before releasing each breath. He went back to his room, showered, and changed clothes to a nice gentleman's attire.

He looked in the mirror while fixing his hair. He then stood back and took one final look then shook his head and left the house.

He walked out to the front of Dave's house. Dave and his girlfriend just arrived and got out of their parked car. Dave moved his head back and looked at Chris then said, "I like your new ride." Two cars were in front of Dave's house, a driver just got out of one and gave the keys to Chris, and he signed a paper and then was given the keys. This man then got into the other car and it drove away. Chris smiled at Dave and said thanks. He walked in the happiest state to this car, a 2019 Bentley Continental GT in deep blue.

He got in started it and sat there with the motor purring for a minute before he drove away saying aloud, "Now, this is more like it." He drove to the most desolate streets of the Vegas strip. He slowed down as he saw two people walking down the sidewalk to the right of him. They were each wearing a face mask. He then lost his smile and his happy composure to the reality of the new state of the city and the world. Stopped at a light, he looked down at the passenger seat and noticed a material object there; it was the same color as the car. He picked it up and saw it was a face mask. He put it on just in time to make the light, though there wasn't any urgency to go as no other car was anywhere around him.

He drove up and down each side of the street, seeing that the famous water towers in front of the Bellagio were turned off- half of the lights of the city were off as well. He then thought to forget about going out to eat. Seeing no other option, he got off of the strip and back on the freeway. He remembered the roads to get to that storage unit where he earlier stopped thinking something suspicious. He stopped about 100 feet before remembering it was at the dead-end of the street.

He lowered his sunglasses, then checked the time on the car clock, then noticed two small cars: one going in and one going out. Each held up a remote then the gate opened for each of them. He thought this is more than unusual as it closed three hours ago. He backed up about twenty feet, and then made a U-turn to leave. While he did this, a large moving van with the same logo as the one he saw earlier was traveling down this dead-end road to that same storage unit. He stopped before making a right to get back onto the road needed to leave this street. Observing in his rear-view mirror, the gate opened for the moving van to go in. He watched this happen then remembered the car that was leaving out the gate and he was very concerned as he no longer saw it. It was more than time to get out of there.

# Chapter 7

JONATHAN WAS IN the dark, cold metal storage locker. He was blindfolded, a cloth was stuck in his mouth and was tied up from shoulder to ankle. Many thoughts went through his mind on how and why this happened. Getting out of there he knew was crucial as the amount of oxygen is diminishing. He then proceeded to the first thing that he knew about getting out of situations like this. He tried moving his arms but it was tight. He grimaced as he relaxed his body gathering full, deep breaths and then started moving his arms, elbows bent like a bird flapping its wings. It had become more than tiring but when he finished each movement, he could feel it loosening. "Persistence. I mean it's not like I have anything else to do."

Now with it somewhat loosened, it still wasn't loose enough to get out of. "I am still wrapped up like a mummy." With each movement that he made to try and free him, he became weaker, both mentally and physically. He stopped at not being able to breathe in any more air. He slumped and curled his body on the cold cement floor.

# Chapter 8

BOND CAME INTO the house sweating from a morning run on the beach. Walking through the house to get to his room, he was surprised to see the nurse had gotten his father out of bed, and now there was another woman in the living room with the three of them. Bond tipped his head to them. He heard this woman say that she did want to speak to him. He told her in 10 minutes he'd be back; he just needed to freshen up first.

While Bond was gone the nurse, Maggie, worked on some motion exercises to get Vincent back into shape. This second woman observed this, but then went through the papers on her lap. Bond made his return dressed in beige pants and a brown polo. He reached open with shaking the woman's hand. She recoiled her body and then told him now that this pandemic has taken a hold of society, distancing must be practiced. He quietly huffed, feeling embarrassed then said aloud to her, "Agreed."

She explained that she was sent from the hospital and that this was just parodical to make sure that everything was going correctly. Jane walked through the room and she smiled to them then took a look at Vincent, then turned around and walked back out. She asked him who Jane was, he explained and gave a summary of her present situation. She then explained to him that she is having a struggle and experiencing grief. She then explained to Bond that there are four phases of grief. Number one is anger.

Bond thought of this and that explained her sudden outbursts to him. The second is rage, within this case he thought it went along with the first. The third is depression then acceptance.

Bond then gathered that she was feeling depressed because of "No Chris" but then she didn't go to him, whereas for acceptance he figured played into this. The therapist then asked him if he had experienced any of these emotions. In his heart, he felt that he did, but this was something that he could never let on to. She then went on further to speak of shock, numbness followed by learning and searching. The third was disorganization and despair; lastly, followed by reorganization and recovery.

He thought that this was a long and involved process, just as he put his head up to look her in the eye. She said to him that she was glad that he understood. He thought, "Can she read my mind?" he then asked her if there were going to be any more visits from her. She explained that the decision would be in the hands of Vincent's doctor. She grabbed hold of her things. Bond walked her to the door and said goodbye.

Bond then went back to Vincent and Maggie in the living room. She smiled at him, and then looked back to Vincent doing these exercises. Bond smiled to his father then looked at him taking it in that his dad wasn't there yet, or was it that his dad will never be the dad that he knew? Calmly taking this new information in, he went into the kitchen. He opened the refrigerator, scoping it out, but not even seeing what was in there. He closed it, then took a banana from the counter and instantly peeled it, then took a bite followed by taking more than a moment to begin chewing it.

With dad, it is more than just a heart attack; he is developing Alzheimer's. This is not what I want, and I don't know what I need…or do I? He then reached inside his pocket, feeling for his car keys and left. He traveled out the gate in the Black SUV and made his way to the coffee shop. Upon parking, he thought it odd that the lot was empty. He looked at the time displayed on the dashboard. "It is most people's lunchtime; the place should be busy.

He got out and saw the back-side door closed. At the front door, it was bolted closed and read a sign saying out of business. Puzzled, he looked up and then thought it's a trap. He felt for his gun, it wasn't there. He stopped only long enough to scope out the area before running back to the SUV.

Starting the engine then looking in the rear-view before backing out he said aloud, "This is getting scary. I am alone, literally this time." He turned left out of the parking lot. "I have no other place to go to, but back home." He was back before he knew it following the roads that he had taken countless times before. Walking out of the open garage, he stopped midsection in the front of the grounds of the estate; he stood back and viewed everything. The separate large garage to the left of the estate was the massive light beige building in the middle of the grounds. This was home; it was where his heart was and is. "It is like the central vein running through my body, my lifeblood." Walking to the front door before turning the knob he speaks out quietly, "I have to save it and the family."

Bond went into the office and then scoured through papers. He leaned back, sighed then drew his clenched hand to his hair and rubbed the side of his head. There has to be a reason that dad had for sending us to Vegas. The only thing that we were told to do was have dinner with the bank President on his identity theft. He again leaned back in the chair, then dropped his body down into the cushion, swirled, and made a surprised look like he just solved Rubik's Cube.

"That is just it! Dad sent us a riddle. Chris and I knew that it was too easy; I mean, why would he send us on something like that? When a bank president in Vegas, would have security beyond..." he paused to scratch behind his ear. "This is ID theft, the whole." He circled his hand in the air. "We are going after a ring of identity thieves.... Another piece of this emerging puzzle solved." He pushed the chair back, "Oh, I am hungry now." He gets up and goes to the kitchen.

In the kitchen, he has various containers, bread, meats, and cheeses on the counter. He notices that Jane came into the kitchen, she is watching him, but she hasn't said anything to him. He felt awkward silence in the air. Mentally he counts down from ten figuring if she hasn't opened up a dialogue; by then, he was counting four, three, at just that moment she sprang into verse. "I haven't seen you too much lately." He pauses while still making his sandwich and wonders in his mind what is "safe" to say to her. He tilts his head then smiled at her.

"I guess, we have both been busy. How are you?" She almost jumped at him in response. "It is not like I haven't been doing anything! I am taking care of Leslie and trying to keep up things around here! It is not like I haven't been doing anything," she walks to the other side of the room with him. He lifts his eyebrows, and then breathes out slowly. Right after he cuts the sandwich in half and puts it on a plate, he asks her if she'd like half. She lets out a breath of air that she'd been holding in then approaches him and looks down to the sandwich. She put her hand forward about to take half then quickly retracts her hand and storms out of the room.

He takes a bite of the sandwich and after swallowing it looks at the empty room and the direction of which she stormed out, and then replies, "Boy, this is fun. I think I'll eat this outside." He picks up the plate in one hand and with the other, he takes a bottle of Stella from the refrigerator and leaves the room. Out on the patio, all is quiet and he savors this. The moon rising in the sky, night setting in, he swears that he can see the light of the moon reflecting on the water. If only for that brief moment he captured tranquility. Finished with the sandwich and the beer, he breathes out, and then rubs his hand down his open thighs pressing in at the kneecaps. "This game has just started… a lot of work ahead. And Jane, her emotions, just has to play it cool…And where did Laurie go?" he gets up and mumbles-back to work.

Back in the office, he takes hold of a piece of paper. He reads it and sets it down, then looks to the ceiling, then to his right, and picks the paper back up, then looks to his left. "Damn it, I didn't read a thing on that page." He takes a burner phone out of the desk drawer and calls Chris; he is already in a firm mood of discontent expecting no answer. On the fourth ring, he hears "hello" from his brother. Bond so surprised by hearing an answer practically drops the phone. Chris can say something wrong, and he asks if everything is okay.

"No, I mean, yes, it is just such a..." "Surprised to hear my voice?" They both laugh. In unison, they say, "I got it." Chris then springs into verse, "Okay, who first?" Bond then opens the conversation. "Dad sent us to Las Vegas to solve a puzzle." Chris then interrupts him, "What?" "Chris, think about it. We meet a bank president on his ID theft."

Chris breaks in, "I know. There is something I found very suspicious at a certain storage facility. Large shipments or large trucks are going in and out after it closes. But what does this have to do with Identity Theft?"

"What is in those shipments?" "This I don't know yet, but I checked into the name on these moving trucks, it is a non-existent business, but it is owned by a medical firm."

"What is the name of this firm?" "Phoenix enterprises," "A medical firm, which is an enterprise. What are they doing?" "This, I am going to find out. I'm going to start by trying to get a job at this storage facility," "Sounds good, well, there is, I say major problem right now." Chris interrupts, "Is Dad okay?" Bond relaxes a bit, "Yes, dad is doing better. But the problem is Jane." Chris takes his hands to his face then presses on each cheek then runs his hand down his neck and drops them. "My wife, God I miss her." "Well, she more than misses you. She is going through a great depression right now, missing you and dad, or shall we say accomplice in who can razz each other the most. I learned from the nurse that there are many stages in this grieving process, and I don't know how much more that she can take." "I know and I am truly sorry, but what else can I or we do, right now?"

"It sounds like we are both doing the necessary things to solve this puzzle." Chris retorts, "Puzzle?" "Relax brother, it is just my analogy of the situation right now" "hey, whatever it takes for you." Bond gets a serious look on his face then slowly tries to relax, "Take Care brother," "You too, bye." He then heard silence and hung up. Then looks over the desk and then wonders how soon and if his dad will ever be able to resume his space there. He tilts his head and makes a smirk, then straightens up in the chair and goes back to work at the desk.

# Chapter 9

PACING BACK AND forth in her bedroom, she stops at each turn she makes. "I am looking for something, but what is it?" She then goes to the side of the bed that is Chris's and very gently and slowly pulls the pillow up from his side of the bed. She gently wraps her arms around it, and then squeezes it crying. "Oh, why? I miss you." In slow, small steps she walks to the window then looks out to the shore. Her crying and stillness stop and rage takes over her body. "Why, why did you leave me, was it something I did? What did I do wrong!!!!!!!!!!!!" she says this screaming. In a torrent of rage, she bounces to the side chair and blunts her body down. "My God, what did I do? I am guilty, but why? I am alone. My only friend is loneliness." She breathes in a short breath and huffs it out then goes to the bed and falls into it sideways.

"I can't hurt anybody when I am not there. When did I go wrong? She then looks up circling the room to see who is watching her again. "Nobody? If I close my eyes, will everything just go away? Can I go back to yesterday? But what part of yesterday?" her cell phone rings, she walks at first slowly, then she increases her speed to get to it on the table. With each passing second, she wonders, who is it? Should she be happy or angry? Is it Chris? Is it going to be Lauren? She eagerly lifts and answers. "Hello," she pauses quietly listening to the voice on the other end of the line. "No, no," she says in anger, "I do not need auto insurance." The voice on the other end continues to talk, she just hangs up.

"Well, at least I am on someone's list." She then grabs for her jacket and goes outside in the night air. The beach, the night is very quiet, she lifts her head to see the moon, and it is half full. She takes steps closer to the direction of it. The other half of it is hiding in the back. She walks to the shoreline and relaxes her body and mind, then stops and looks down at her footprints in the sand. There is only one set of footprints, usually there are two. "Bond, I suppose things will never be the same for us."

"What am I going to do now?" She walks back to the house and grabs a bottle of wine from the kitchen and a glass then goes back to the patio. She sits down and pours herself a full glass, then stops to look at it before raising it in the air. "Here is to you, Moon." Then proceeds to a full sip followed by many more. She then wonders if she'll finish it and replies to herself, "Probably. But will I find myself out here in the morning or wake up in my bed? I don't seem to have my savior anymore. I'll be out here."

Chris stops at a 7-11 and gets a 12 pack of Stella, some hot dogs, and buns, while waiting until his turn, he sets them on the counter, and then jumps a little surprised. The clerk makes note of him and shows an angry face, thinking that he left his money in the car. Chris runs to the side aisle and comes back with a jar of mustard. He pays for them, and then drives back to Dave's place. No, I need to make one more stop before returning home. He circles then make his way back to the freeway then exits to the storage facility.

Stopped at the entrance gate and not having the code, he presses the button on the metal box and makes an explanation, ten seconds later the gate opens. He stops only to tuck in his shirt before going inside the office. A small-framed man with a graying black balding hairline looks up to him as he enters.

"There is a pamphlet there on the counter, on the fees and the unit sizes. And right now, I only have one 8 by 8 available." Chris opens the conversation in a very calm manner and gentle voice and explains to him that he was just looking for a job, his wife has just left him and because of this current pandemic, he lost his job. He just stopped there to see if any employee might be available there. This man behind the counter looked down, then up to view Chris's face dead in the eye. "I need somebody right now. BUT not for the office, this is my job. I need someone for maintenance…like janitorial work. I know that you wouldn't have any experience in that." He then scratches the top of his head.

Chris smiles and shows uplifted joy. "As a matter of fact, I do have some experience as a school janitor. I know, I mean this is much different from my last job, but Sir, right now I desperately need something." The man looks down at the counter, then takes out a set of keys and a 4 by 4-inch notebook from the drawer and throws the keys to Chris and hands him the notebook. "You're hired, be here at 8 tomorrow morning." Chris smiles and thanks him then walk out the door, "Wait a minute." Chris drops his face. "What is your name?" At that second, he froze, he couldn't give him his real name and anything that would lead to his identity. He was caught in a whirlwind, and he moved his head briefly shaking for a second and then blurted out, "Dave… Okay, then Dave be on time tomorrow."

"I will." He smiles at him again and then asks for his name. This man answered while looking at the time clock, "Larry." Chris then leaves smiling and drives back to Dave's place.

While driving him notices that the traffic has greatly lightened up, and again he knows from the pandemic. He then wonders what the course of this work will be. "I will have to get a new mask that is for sure. There is probably the one back home. Home, Jane." He drops his composure after saying this while waiting for the gate to open. He parks then go to the kitchen. "Hot dogs and beer, what could be better?"

# Chapter 10

THE MORNING SUN shined bright through drifting clouds; a light breeze, then blew on a beautiful Hawaiian morning. On the outside patio of the estate, Bond walked holding a cup of coffee to the table. Jane had her head and the upper body lay over the patio table. He thought that he saw her move but heard only silence.

"Good morning," she moved her head up and grimaced in pain. She then opened and closed her eyes, trying to figure everything out. "I brought you coffee." He placed it down on the table in front of her. She lightly started to shake her head in appreciation, and then stopped moving. In soft words, she said thank you.

"Must have been a nice night that you slept here," he then smiled at her. She took the cup to her mouth holding it in both hands and took a small sip. "I-I, ah, the coffee is good." She opened her mouth to speak to him again, then swallowed hard and raised her eyebrows then quickly wobbled out of the chair and ran inside to the bathroom. Bond looked to the table and raised the empty wine bottle. "All of it? I hope she made it there in time."

Back inside the house he didn't see her and didn't see any signs of what the outcome might have been, he was happy with that note. He then heard what he thought was a cry of pain, he walked to this noise. It came from his father's room. He didn't see Maggie there. He then saw the side bathroom door slightly open and a light came from it. He quickly went there very concerned about what he would find. His father was wrapped in a bath towel; the room was still steamy from the shower. His father then sideways eyed Bond and saw his questioning look. "Nobody is going to take a blade to my face, but me." Vincent held a tissue to a small cut he had made shaving. Bond knew better to say anything to him on the matter.

He just held his lips closed and left.

Now inside the office, he thought to himself, well dad is getting better. Another piece on the puzzle board moved. He stopped in his movement on the work on his laptop on the desk. Something just does not feel right, what is going on in Vegas? Chris…Jonathan, I hope that you are okay, both of you. He lowered his head back to his work on the desk. This whole thing…I should be there, what am I doing here? A puzzle piece is out of place. Hearing the noise of the door open he looked for it. Vincent stood there at the open door, "I'm back." An instant smile came to both of their faces as Bond got up from behind the desk.

Bond got up and went to his father then helped him to the chair behind the desk. "So, tell me has everything gone as planned, or did you two mess things up?" Bond sat opposite his father and listened to this. "You, planned this?" "The two of you had to figure out that I wouldn't send you on just identity theft of a banker, of all people?" Bond squirmed in the chair. "That, I figured out. There is something a lot more serious than identity theft going on and Chris seems to be on top of it." Vincent nodded his head. "What about Jane?" Bond again squirmed in the chair then raised his posture. "Jane. What about Jane?" "How are you to doing and does Chris miss her and does she miss him?" Bond starts to say something, but seems to stale for time, Vincent then interrupts him, "What about blabbermouth, where is she?" Bond then laughs as Vincent does as well.

Bond filled Vincent in on everything that he had found out so far. After hearing all that he needed to hear, he nodded his head. Silence filled the room for not even a minute before he told Bond, "What are you waiting for. Vegas is calling." Bond got up, and then went to his room to pack; most things that he did pack were already packed for the move, as he was anticipating it. He wondered what he should say to Jane, after much thinking about it, he decided that nothing was better than the wrong thing, now it was a matter of getting out of there without her seeing it. He then thought she is nursing a hangover and probably be in her bedroom for most of the day.

When he left his room now at the entry to the house, Vincent was there at the open door. A stretch limo was parked in the portico with the back door open, waiting for Bond. Bond grabbed a tighter hold of his bag, then nodded to Vincent and told him to take care then got in the limo and it took off for the airport.

Vincent went to the outside patio a guard by his side; he looked out to the ocean and watched the tide pull back and forth. He said quietly to himself, "It is good to be back."

# Chapter 11

I N LAS VEGAS while deboarding a direct flight from Hawaii to Vegas Bond looked sleepy. He stopped at a coffee stand in the airport before going to the gate to get his bag. He noticed that a few people caught his eye; he then wondered was this tiredness that he felt or being in a new place, or the uncertainty of what was to happen next. He then deduced- all of the above.

Now outside the airport and the business and noise, he swore that his mind stopped on what to do next. He stopped and got out his phone hearing a beep. He answered it was Chris. All he said was, "Blue Bentley." Bond scoured the area in front of him, and then saw it across the next aisle of cars. He checked the traffic, and then ran with it. He opened the door and got in. Chris wearing his sunglasses smiled at him, "Nice trip here?" Bond finished snapping his seat belt on and replied, "Oh, the best." They both laughed and then proceeded back to Dave's.

Now miles from the airport, Bond noticed the nearly barren streets and freeways. Chris looked over at him and sensed this, "Want to see something amazing?" Bond made no verbal response just lightly shook his head. Now on the nearly vacant famed Vegas strip, Bond looked puzzled and somewhat bewildered by the lack of anything there. "I suppose that I have lived in my world, for a while now, that I did not realize the severity of the matter. My God…" Chris turned the vehicle into a side street, then speed up to make it back to the freeway. "Yes, bad for us in solving this case but…" he slowed down to turn the car and made a brief pause, then resumed speech, "But especially bad for mankind and the world." Bond breathed out heavily in response. He softly said in a quiet voice, "A plague to mankind."

Walking in the front door of Dave's place, Bond puts his bag down; Chris took his dark glasses off, and then went to the kitchen. He took a bottle of Stella from the fridge and asked Bond if he wanted one. "Chris, you know I don't drink, but right now, the answer is yes." He took it from him, and then had trouble turning the cap, Chris grabbed it and turned it, releasing the cap then handed it back to Bond.

They sat at the table in the kitchen instead of going outside to the backyard to sit. Right now, they each felt that they wanted security. Chris mentioned to Bond that it was great that father was back. Bond replied, shaking his head. "But right now, we have no direction from him, it is up to us." Chris took a swallow then shook his head, "Pressure." Bond responded, "Yeah, a lot of it sounds to me though that you have some idea of something going on." Chris shook his head in response then poured out everything that he knew to Bond on the situation. Chris only stopped once to take a pizza from the refrigerator and place it in the oven.

They ate in silence. Now finished they cleaned up after themselves then went into their bedroom. Bond got all unpacked then took a shower and relished the pulsating jets, relieving tension in his back and shoulders. Finished with the shower, he left the bathroom wearing dark blue sweatpants and a loose white tee shirt. He breathed in then let out a deep quiet sigh, "I need something, for the first and so far, the only time in my life, I feel this way." He bent down further, still sitting on the edge of the bed. He rose to perfect from hearing a knock on the door. A moment later, Chris came in; he noticed the sunken-in-feeling coming from his brother, "Are you alright?"

"Right now? Well, I have been better." "I am just asking, did Jane tell you to say anything to me?" At that moment he wondered if he should tell him the truth or extend a pleasant lie. Then he quickly made up his mind to tell the truth because his brother could always sense if something wasn't quite right. "Sorry, Chris, she didn't, but she is in a very deep sense of loss and denial right now." Chris dropped his face, and then dropped his body instantly. "She is, is she depressed?" "Sorry but that and more." Chris stood there silent. Bond combed his mind for what to do finding no answer, he remained silent. "She is depressed- things will get better or be better when I am back." "Yes, brother they certainly will. Good night." He turned his head and slowly closed the door behind him, and mumbled out, "Good night."

Bond got up from the corner of the bed and reached into the bathroom just enough to turn the light off. He then went to the side of the bed and turned down the bed covers on his side. Before getting into the bed he visually circled the room then opened his mouth and tilted his head. "This will be home for I don't know how long." He then got in under the covers. "I guess that I am safe in one regard but in more than another there is just uncertainty, hence the job, but not the state of the world." He reached over and turned off the bed lamp then looked for any shadow in the room. "Nothing," he rolled over and over tossing and turning finally stopping, "Laurie". He then fell into a deep needed sleep.

The following morning, he showered then dressed casually for the day. He was led into the kitchen with the beautiful aroma of freshly brewed coffee. He stopped at the counter in front of the coffee pot and thought, the maid is back. Pouring himself a cup of this morning elixir he heard footsteps approach him. He was very relaxed on hearing this though because he could recognize it was his brother's footsteps. Chris handed him some half and a half for the coffee. He asked Chris if the maid was back. Chris responded, "No, I made it." Bond tilted his head and then commented to him that it was good.

They both sat down, Bond took a sip as Chris handed him the morning newspaper. Bond took it, opening it to read. "The whole city is on lockdown." He breathed out and waited for a response from Bond. Hearing nothing from him, he started speaking again, "We have to come up with a plan. I checked and the storage facility is still open, not affected by the closure, yet." "Well, you told me you have a job there now, don't you?" "Yes, I do, but what will you be doing while I am working? Watching soap operas?" Bond choked on his swallow at hearing that remark.

"No, I'm pretty up to date on them, except for as the World turns." Chris huffed a smile and replied, "Is that still on?" Bond replied to him, "You seemed to have calmed down from your normal self." "It is called working without a plan." He then lifted the saltshaker from the table and looked at intensely while turning it. Bond licked his lips then remarked, "Somehow I think that we are going to fall into the plan." They paused for the same amount of time then remarked in unison, "father". They both got up and commented to each other that they better get the day started.

Going out the door Chris gave the keys to the Bentley to Bond, and he took the Toyota to work commenting that driving the Bentley there just wouldn't look right. Bond nodded, then waited for Chris to leave out the gate then followed him to the freeway. Bond saw Chris depart on an exit and kept going thinking that he still did not know what to look for. He then thought just to observe anything that is out there. "What could be open, but grocery stores and some gas stations?" taking the next turning viewing, a large building complex, "hospitals. Shall I be Marcus Welby? Or George Clooney on e.r.? What was his name?"

Now parked in the hospital lot which surprised him as being very full. He then rationalized, the pandemic people going there with symptoms, wanting the immediate outcome. He looked in the rear-view mirror examining his face and thinking still, what am I doing? He thought about how once before years ago, he played the part of a doctor in Italy when trying to solve a case in Florence. Closing the door, he thought, no Italian accent needed here. But there I had my entourage right there with me, this time I'm solo. He stopped in fear and fright showing on his face, then opened the door back up and reached for it then put on his face mask.

Inside at the e.r. entrance, he went to the window; there was a line of people so long that he stopped counting at 15. He thought Personnel; he followed steps of white medical jackets, trying to look like he knew where he was going. He stopped for what he thought sneeze, which was now dead to do, but they need to sneeze which turned into a long yawn, he still took his hand to cover the facial mask while doing this. Coming out of the yawn turns his face to the right and he saw the sign marked "Personnel", he thought today is my lucky day. He went inside the busy office and explained to or tried to explain to two clerks there each responding to phone calls and viewing the medical staff going and coming out of the swinging doors behind them. He saw the Oriental man that just hung up the phone and entered information onto the computer screen in front of him. He flashed a badge to him and said that he was Doug ross from Chicago General. He was there on vacation but found the need to help.

The clerk took a minute out of his busy schedule and thanked him, then pointed to the swinging doors behind him. "Doug ross from Chicago?! Straight out of e. r. I suppose Clooney is behind you. Go now, we needed you hours ago." Bond proceeded through the doors and grabbed a white lab coat off the coat rack to the side of the wall. A name was printed on it; he didn't even take the time to read the name or even see that there was a name printed on it. He leaned his body against the wall to make room for the running stuff. Some sort of emergency he thought. He used his skill to blend in and then made it to the third floor where the labs were located.

Various workers have conducted last work on blood samples, and they were also looking at the samples through microscopic machines. He walked down behind each row of workers. A man in a white lab coat yelled to him, "haven't you brought me that Sanders result yet." He looked to him then down to the workers in front of him. He was then handed the papers result from a worker. "It is awful the way the computer system of the hospital slowed down and we have to do things the old way at the moment." He walked to this man and gave him the results. He then quickly walked back from the direction that he came. He tried opening a large metal door to the backside of the room. An attendant quickly went to him and replied to him while placing his hand and stopping him from opening this door.

"You know that is the controlled cold room for organs. I suppose in all of this commotion you probably forgot." Bond instantly smiled at him and thanked him. He waited until this man left then he sidestepped quickly out of the room. He followed the signs to the cafeteria but did not go into the room while in motion he took off the lab coat. A janitor wheeled his cart in the opposite direction that he was walking, and he dropped it in that cart, then made his way back to the parking lot and his car.

Driving out of the lot he thinks to himself, have I found the next lead to pursue or, do I need to check out the other three hospitals in the Las Vegas Area. He accelerates as the streetlight turns green, then says aloud, "Yes,

I have to check them all out. I just hope that things are going well for dad." Boy, I am thirsty; stopping anywhere other than a grocery store is no risky as most eating places have been shut down. "Ah, there to the right liquor store." He turns into the lot and parks, now inside he reached for a Pepsi then grabs two glasses of water as well. He fumbles nearly dropping one trying to balance the three in his hands. A group of men standing in line in front of him turns to look at him. Feeling embarrassed, he just gives them a light smile. He then thought it odd with the heat of Vegas daytime that they all except for the one in front and into the middle were wearing heavy jackets that had an emblem sewed in the middle of the back of the jacket.

It is now this group's turn at the counter again. He hears laughter and then the voice of the clerk saying that they must be having a celebration hence the champagne. And two 12 packs of Bud, this must be the chaser. Again, laughter filled the air. He watches taking everything in but just as the one to the front of the man in the middle turned his head to him, Bond takes tissue from his pocket then fakes a sneeze. "Come on, we got to get out of here." Bond watches then leave the building and then go into a large van larger than the average passenger van. The clerk watches him and looks annoyed. Bond apologizes, then pays for the soda and the water, thanks him and leaves.

Now out in the parking lot, he sees this large van turn out of the parking lot and he memorizes the plate. Once inside his car, he enters the plate number on his phone. He only stays here long enough to drink half of the Pepsi then turns out of the lot and heads north for the two hospitals there. "I guess that I am playing doctor today."

# Chapter 12

A T THE STORAGE facility, Chris checks it with Larry at the office. Larry hands him the necessary paperwork to fill out a series of information, social security number, address, family. Chris freezes when he reads this. Larry lifts his head to him, "What is the matter, are you illegal or something?" Chris then relaxes his composure. "No, it is not that. It is just that…" Larry starts to gruff. Chris picks up on this, "Well, it is my wife, remember I told you that I am going through a divorce right now and if she finds out of the income that I am making here she'll want some of that too." Larry softens his composure, "eight dollars an hour cash and I say nothing." Chris starts to smile then stops, "how about ten?" Larry breaths in lifting his head then lower his head and say, "Nine and no more, and no benefits." Chris lifts his hand and replies, "Yes." Larry then hands him the keys to the electric cart and a broom, mop, pail, and cleaning supplies, then tell him that the restrooms have to be cleaned and anywhere else that needs to be swept. Chris reaches for these items with a cracked smile, and then goes outside of the cart places the supplies in the cart and leaves to find the restrooms. He says in his mind, I have been through worse. Through never-ending countless minutes, he leaves the men's restroom and places the supplies back in the cart. He wipes his forehead with the cotton fabric of his shirt. "Oh, I am glad that's finished." He rides around the grounds getting his bearings, as to where everything is, there are two second-story storage units and he remembered that Larry told him not to worry about one of them. It was leased out to a business.

He thinks he should leave it alone until he can establish trust with Larry. What is in there? There has to be a connection to it and the large moving vans going in and out of here at all hours. If I check it out now, it could just be - I'm new and this is my naivety. He parks and then takes hold of the broom and walks all around the outside of the building. He stops to sweeps whenever necessary. At the backside of this unit, he stops seeing the door and knowing that no one was watching him. He takes the large circular key ring containing about twenty keys to the lock. He takes hold of one key and starts to place it inside of the lock then stops upon hearing a car motor coming toward him. He takes back hold of the broom and starts sweeping again. A car door, then slams; he fights from all of this training to run and instead stays there reluctant to move.

The sound of footprints comes closer to him. He clenches the broom hands harder, thinking he can attack with the swipe or a broom. A soft voice of an elderly woman then is heard. She only wants directions. He clenches his shoulders tighter then drops his body to relax, smiles and then walks around to the front of the building and tries to tell her where she is looking for. He sees that she just looks further confused. So, he gets in his cart and tells her to follow him. She does and then thanks him after they got where she needed to go.

A reddish faded thirty years old Chevy pickup then stops by the side of him. The side window rolls down and he sees that it is Larry. "I have to go out. I locked the office and put up a sign as to when I'll be back. If anyone asks, just tell them that we are full and if they need to make a payment, they can just drop it in the slot or call back later." He nods his head then watches this old man and truck leave. He asks the woman if she is okay now, she says yes, and he loves going right back to that two-story unit.

In quiet uniformity he goes one by one holding the keys on the ring and then finds the right one on the twelfth, he raises his eyebrows and smiles in his mind saying "Bingo". Standing back from the strong odor exhumed from the now open building, he steps back and covers his mouth. He stands back still while looking at the dark inside of the building. He walks forward still covering his mouth and nose, and then stands still and quiet, just one foot inside. "It smells like rotting meat, did something die in here?" he goes back to the cart and searches through the toolbox. He goes back to the open door holding a flashlight.

Stepping inside the metal and wood building, he stops releasing his hand from his mouth takes a deep breath and turns on the flashlight and decides on whether to go to the left or the right being a solid wall block the middle of the inside. He takes the left, shining the flashlight down the empty silent wide hallway. Toward the end of the hall, there are doors to each side. He observes a code and a padlock are on each door. A small hallway led to the other side of the building and in just shinning the flashlight down the other hallway he sees that it is the same thing. The upstairs, how do you get to the upstairs?

Standing there silent, he can find no other option but to go down the right side. Again, he has to cover his mouth and nose from the intense foul odor. Carefully and quietly walking down the hall, he feels that is going to surprise an animal. What kind of animal worries him and he more than anything wishes that he could be able to reach for his gun. It feels like I am the pawn in a trap. The last door on the right side is an elevator. He looks for the key latch to open it, there isn't one. To his surprise, it is just the standard push-button on public elevators. He shyly reaches for it and pushes it in waiting for an alarm to go off and run. There is a ding and then the doors open, it is lit inside. It feels like it is waiting for me. He enters and then presses the top button, a brief pause and the door closes. He didn't even feel the jarring stop; he gets out and then makes a piercing view of all of the surroundings. The same as below, only you can only go one way to the left. He walks down looking at each side with each passing step. The shrill quickness of the place overwhelmed him. Now at the end of the hall, there is just one small unit and another locked door, he presumes to get to the other side of the building. That one smaller unit was the only thing that is different and he wonders why. There is only a small code lock on this unit where all the others had two separate locks. He bends down to the lock and sees the indentations in the roll-up door. He then looks both surprised and a bit fearful then composes himself listening more. There is a small noise. In the stillness and quietness of this building, the sound of even a mouse would seem like a roar. It is like he can hear a human being giving his last breath. Listening for any other sign of life to what the identity of this is he hears a faintly audible voice. He gets up examining whether he hears a sound coining toward him. I fear being caught, he instantly decided to leave. Before going he made a small voice to the door, "Jonathan, (he thinks if that is you) I'll be back soon, I'm sorry, but I have to go." He moves as fast as a deer and quickly as a jackal to the elevator. The seconds count endlessly for the door to open. At the bottom he runs in the same quick precision as before, making it outside he doesn't even turn around before locking it back up. Now standing with his back to the door, he doesn't see anything, but something just does not feel right.

The first thing that he does do is to make it back to where he had earlier left the older woman to see if she was alright. She was gone, so he rides around the perimeter of the grounds to check on anything and everything. All was clear, there was still, something just did not seem right. He drove back to the office, went inside and bought a can of soda and a bag of Dorito's from the vending machine, then sat on a chair for customers to speak or talk with the manager. Just as he swallowed a sip of the lemon-lime soda, the front door opened, and his boss came in.

He replied, "Caught you!" Chris then replied to him that he just now stopped for his break/lunch. Larry then told him that he better make it quick because if a customer does come in, he'll have to leave. He nodded his head. "I am going to use the can," he places a folded pamphlet on the counter, and then goes to the rest room. Chris takes one last sip of the soda, then crumbles the chip bag and goes behind the counter to throw them away. He lifts the pamphlet to read what it is. It was a horse racing form. That explains his long lunches out. He goes back to the other side of the counter, looks out the window and waits for him to return to get the next instruction on what to do.

On the latest instruction from Larry, he finds himself at the back of the office and the equipment garage building to repair a tear in the cyclone fence. He stretches out the loose fence and sees where to put the bolts, then forms the escape. He uses only plastic ties to seal it is giving the appearance of being fixed, but remaining useful, useful to him anyway. He spends the rest of the day doing the ordinary until the workday ended. Now each of them in their cars, he waits for Larry's to start his engine before leaving.

One turn, two turns, three turns, Larry's engine won't start. Chris then exasperated gets out of his car and goes to Larry and his truck.

He can see Larry's anger; he then asks Larry for the keys so he can try. I just turned the key and I could see it plain and simple, Larry was out of gas. He got out and told Larry of this. It sounded like the language of a drunken sailor. Chris got out and then offered Larry a ride home or to a gas station to get fuel. Larry opted for ride home. Chris was surprised at Larry's home, it was just a typical apartment complex, and with the persona of Larry he imagined him in an old farmhouse. Larry got out and didn't even turn to him to thank him.

The only thing to do now is going home, home, Jane. This not home here, but it has to be for the meantime anyway. He made it to the freeway and relaxed to a CD by Taylor Dayne as he drove. He didn't care if he could be seen singing or pounding his wrist on the steering, but for that moment it was a release, a much needed and welcomed release.

# Chapter 13

NSIDE THE GATES of Dave's estate, he saw Bond's car or his Bentley was already there. The garage was left open, he presumed for him.

He waited until he could see the last bit of the door close, and then went inside. He could smell something simmering and it smelled good. He didn't see Bond and no one answered his call. rather than check his bedroom, he looked out to the patio, sure enough, that is where he was, sitting at the table with a bottle of Stella and one was there waiting for Chris.

"You know, you are getting good at this, pretty soon you'll make a nice wife." He lightly punched Chris after that remark. Between swallows of beer, they told each other the outcomes of their days and work that night had been gone over. They nodded to each other, got up and then went to the kitchen. Bond made Chicken Parmigiana and wilted spinach with warm Italian Bread. Both of them went right into eating and enjoying their meal. After cleaning up in the kitchen, they each went to their room, showered and changed clothes to ready for that night.

Bond went out to the front and saw Chris running around the lot. He presumed to get his body charged for the coming events. He ran over to Bond. "We both have to take separate cars, but…, not the Bentley. Here are the keys to his jeep, use that and you know where to meet me." Bond caught the keys and they each left for the storage facility. There was still a slight pit of sunlight in this summer evening. Bond noticed on the drive there that overhead clouds were darkening the sky, which was great news for them. Chris slowed down at the side of the facility and nodded his head then pointed out that this is where Bond needed to stop. He did and just waited in the parked car, to the side of the cyclone fence under a tree.

Chris drove around to the front entrance of the storage facility, he swiped his head in every direction, and then got out of the Toyota, but instead of punching the code at the gate and using his key, he went to the backside where Bond waited. Seeing his brother approach on the left side of the fence, Bond got out. They went to the opening and broke the zip ties that Chris had put there earlier. Before entering Bond whispered, "Alarm?" Chris whispered back that he turned it off before he left with the drunken boss. He nodded to him before they went inside. even though there were various outside lights at the facility, it was still dark at the entrance door to the building. Chris flashed the light from his key chain at the lock.

Chris punched the code of the lock, and then used the key from the office to open the door. It did not unlock. Bond grimaced seeing this outcome and Chris expelled a look of fright. Bond then moved closer to Chris and took the keys. He turned the ring of keys to his face then pinched one together and placed it in the lock. He stopped when it went in, but he didn't turn it. Chris looked at him like what are you waiting for. Being the trained spy, Bond was listening for the clicking of a bomb that was sometimes rigged to "special" doors. Hearing only silence for those ever slow passing seconds he then proceeded, turn, and the lock is now open. They both breathed a silent sigh of relief and then ran inside the building with Chris in the lead holding the flashlight.

Instead of using the elevator afraid that this might trigger something, they climbed the fire ladder just feet away from the side of the elevator. Chris had climbed more than the needed steps to get off on that floor. He stopped his body on the step, clenched his fingers on the ladder, then jumped down and rolled off on the floor with the precision and quietness of a cat. Bond watched this and just stepped off walking down the hall following Chris. Now in front of the door where Jonathan was being held, Chris proceeded to cut the lock, Bond tapped his shoulder and Chris looked at him. Bond then pointed at a tripwire on the side of the door. Chris thought that he had thoroughly checked this out and not seen it.

This means that someone had been there and unnoticed. Was Jonathan still in there and was he alive?

Bond took out a switchblade and opened it cutting the wire. Time was of the essence, there was most certainly a silent alarm attached to it. They looked at each other nodded then opened the door. Bond stood back and held the door open. Chris ran to the coiled-up figure in the middle of the floor. It didn't move, he touched feeling of heat. It was cold and lifeless. He placed the body over his shoulder, and then ran out of the door that Bond was holding open, the door now was trying to push closed at resistance.

Bond exerted a cry of pain using all of his strength to keep it open as Chris was now crossing over the threshold of the door. Successfully, Chris made it out with the body over his shoulder, he did not stop to view his brother who was still in a fight with the closing door. Chris was now halfway down the hall leading to the elevator. Bond again grimaced in pain and he was out, but his shirt was caught between the doors. He tried ripping it off, it wouldn't tear. He then closed his eyes then lowered his head and body, raised his arms and got the shirt off. He did not slow himself in any respect and was now right behind his brother.

In front of the elevator Bond pushed the button for it to open; even if they had been discovered there was no way that the body could be carried down the stairs. It opened on the bottom floor, it looked clear so they exited and then opened the door and left the building. Chris then ran the body to the gate opening then placed it on top of Bond's shoulder. Bond ran the body and placed it in the Jeep. Chris went back inside of the facility and locked the door and code box back up. Running back to the entrance where he parked his car, he heard a loud siren and then flashing red lights that strobe through the grounds of the facility.

Now with the body lay out on the back seat of the Jeep, Bond could see Jonathan's face. He continued to loosen the wrappings around his chest. Bond then said his name, "Jonathan, Jonathan, you are safe. It is me, Bond." The head lightly moved. "No, no, be still." He moved his ear to Jonathan's mouth, and then raised and looked at his torso; his chest seemed that it caved in. Bond stopped only for an instant hearing the sirens. He then reached under the passenger seat for a leather bag, opened it, and then placed oxygen in Jonathan. Jonathan breathed in and then again.

A small cough was heard then Jonathan opened his eyes. He looked at Bond in a questioning fashion, Bond knew that he was confused, but he also knew the urgency to get out of there. He fastens the seat belt under Jonathan and then got in and drove away from the scene. He heard Jonathan moan, but then knew that he could now do nothing about it. He drove up the block and then made a legal U-turn, drove through another four lights, then pulled in the parking lot of a 7-11. He parked in the side back of the lot where he thought there could have only been employee's cars parked. He got out and again checked on Jonathan. He felt his pulse then nodded his head to him. "You will get better buddy." He gave Jonathan an open bottle of water. "Take it easy there and drink it slowly." Jonathan opened and closed his eye to him and took two small sips then lightly nodded to him. "I know you will get better." He rose up his body standing to the side of the open back door of the Jeep and then actually felt a car driven by him. Without moving his head, he circled his eyes to the motion of this car. It drove right past him and seemed in a planned course. He moved his hand over his hair and then faked a sneeze to look in the direction that it traveled as it just parked. He saw a middle-aged man exit the car. The man walked to the back of the dark building that had a very small flashlight size, light shining over a sign above the door. He smiled at the door, then the door opened. He could see a woman's head on the door then closed and both were inside. This was out of what the course that he should do for that evening, but the curiosity got the better of him. He walked to the end side of the lot and then strained his eyes to read what was written on the sign. He opened and contracted his pupils, then made out that the sign said "Lucky's Bar". He then smiled, well society needs a release right now, and speaking of that we'd better get out of here, he seems to be better.

He walked back to the open back door, smiled at Jonathan and told him that they're going home. He could see the fear instantly expressed over Jonathan's face. "We, you and I are going to my home, not yours." Hearing this Jonathan smiled then seemed to relax in the seat. Bond was glad to see this. He then got in and slowly left the parking lot.

At the storage facility, Chris stopped his run and then just took the flashlight from his key ring and shinned it over the asphalt grounds of the facility. He could see the lights from two police cars approaching him. The officers from both cars and Larry the manager of the facility all got out and started walking toward him. He looked up to them and expressed a look of fright and concern. An officer then yelled out, "freeze, drop down to the ground." He did show panic in his eyes. Two of the officers then ran directly to him, one in front and the other in the back of him, handcuffing him. He was then told to stand as the officer in the back of him helped him up.

Larry walked forward now standing just ten feet in front of Chris. "You, you work for me, I trusted you." Chris lowered his face showing shame and then pleaded like a puppy seeking forgiveness for chewing up an owner's slipper. "I had to come back, you see." "Oh, I see a lot right now." "No, please let me explain." Larry opened his mouth to proceed in dialogue and the officers that stood to his side stopped him. Then an officer standing in front of Chris said, "let's hear him out."

In an almost laughing voice he responded to them, "I got home then I realized that I forgot my wristwatch. It wasn't in my place or my car. I panicked, Doretha, my wife who was going to divorce me called me and told me that she might give me another chance, and asked to meet me tomorrow. I couldn't show up and not have on the wristwatch that she gave me...I mean, I am lost without her and I just want her back." He made a brief pause, the officers moved their heads wanting to hear more of the story; Larry just had a look of extreme annoyance over his face and body. "I came back to look for it." The officer standing to the side of Larry asked him, "The wristwatch?"

The officer to the side of him then bent over and picked up something from the asphalt and he lifted it. The officer that stood in front of Chris then walked over to him and took the watch. He held it in front of Chris and said, "This is what you were looking for?" he then tried to place it on Chris's wrist, it fits perfectly. And the pin went right in the latch. The officer then lowered his pad, "Come on, there is nothing for us to do here." He then asked Larry if there was any money on the grounds. They all paused while

Chris stood there still with handcuffs on as Larry opened the office and checked the safe, nothing had been tampered with.

The two of them then locked the office. Outside while an officer took the handcuffs off of Chris, Larry yelled out, "You're fired and give me the keys right now!" The officer to the side of Chris waited for him to give him the keys then the officer handed them to Larry.

After that, an officer accompanied Chris to his Toyota that was parked right in front of the entrance gates. Chris got in then waited a minute and started the car and drove away. Driving away, Chris thought, why didn't they question me on how I got inside the gate? He smirked and entered the freeway. And merged into medium flow traffic and headed home.

# Chapter 14

NOW PARKED AT Dave's he felt uneasy walking inside the home, the feeling that you get when someone is watching you and you don't know why or who, or for what reason. He then thought of the day and the only thing that he now wanted to do was go inside, kick off his shoes, change into his sweats and grab a beer. That he did and just hearing Bond's voice inside, he felt an even tone to life at that moment. Going inside the kitchen and pulling out a beer, he was disappointed on not smelling anything cooking, instead of walking outside as he planned to, he followed steps leading him to where his brother's voice became louder.

It came from Dave's master bedroom; he then thought an intrusion to the man that owns this place. He gently opened the door then saw Jonathan in the bed, Bond stands by his side and a doctor standing to the side of him. Chris then lowered his composure to the situation. Bond saw Chris there and then told him of the matter. "Doctor Willis, this is my brother Chris, (they each nodded to the other) he checked on Jonathan and gave me a course, or the US a course to follow, for his recovery." The doctor then grabbed his bag and left. Chris walked over to Bond and stood beside the bed. Jonathan looked at Chris and smiled. He smiled back in return. Bond then looked down at Jonathan, and told him to rest, the two of them then left for the kitchen.

Bond sat first, Chris held up his beer and then offered to get one for Bond, and he declined. Bond started the conversation, "There is a lot that I've found out." Chris turned his head wanting to know more about this, then sat down and gave his attention to Bond. "I have talked with father." He stopped and breathed out a sigh. "It seems that we are being watched. There is a drone that flies above the house and grounds." Chris starts to talk; Bond takes back the control of the conversation. "I know, what enemies do we have? Or could this just be a crazy fan of Dave who wants to know or see more of him? And it seems that the paper trail of what Jonathan did or has found out is gone. Everything is missing from his condo. We are going up against something bigger than a gang. Father does not think that the police know anything about this. He has arranged for Jonathan to be flown back to Hawaii- maybe when he gets better, the two of them can work on things." Chris then replied to Bond, "This leaves us pawns on the chessboard."

"Again, father saw this, he has arranged for a 'man' to come and help us." Chris quipped, "help us?" "This person knows everything about Las Vegas and shall I say dealings. Oh, and he is also a movie double." "An actor, oh, that is going to help us." The doorbell rings. They both get up to answer it, Bond remains calm, but Chris is apprehensive on "who" is there.

Bond pulls the door open; Chris is surprised while Bond nods his head to this man and waves his hand for him to enter. He is holding his leather suitcase in one hand and a bag of Chinese food in the other. When the door is closed, more smiles are made. "I brought dinner. I hope that you haven't eaten yet." "No, we need it." Bond then shows him the guest room to the side back of the kitchen, he goes on and Chris takes the food bag to the kitchen and sets it everything on the table. Bond is drawn to the living room, suspicious of something. The drone is flying visible as he stands in the middle of the room. He takes a remote from the side end table by the couch, pushes a button and a panel closes blocking off all view of the window, the room instantly darkens. He adjusts his eyes before trying to make his way back to the kitchen. He checks on Jonathan; he is asleep, he then smiles and goes back to the kitchen.

The guest comes back to the kitchen where they all sit and start digging into the food. He looks over to Chris and replies, "I know what you are thinking, and I heard your earlier reply after seeing me." Bond starts to say something, and then the guest interrupts him, "I look like the actor Thomas Jane. I am his double on the movie set anyway." "Is that why you are here and he is in California?" "Right now, I don't know if California or not. But as you can imagine mostly everything in the film business has come to a halt with this virus." Bond takes the conversation, "I do have a question for you?" he stops to wipe his mouth with a napkin. "What is your name?" They all laugh. "My name is Troy, Troy Benson."

Through the course of dinner, they went through the dealings of what they knew so far. Both Chris and Bond give Troy a heads up on their father's works. After dinner's over Troy goes to his room, then Bond and Chris make a sweep of the house. They gather back in the middle of the hallway 15 minutes later. "All the windows are covered, the doors are air tight, the garage is closed and the gate is locked and the alarm is on… I do not know how we could make this place any more secure, with maybe the exception of Zeus and Apollo." They laughed at this made reference to the two-guard dogs on the "Magnum P.I." TV series.

"Call father." "It's late." "It is an earlier time there, remember." Bond then wonders about Chris, he didn't say anything, but he thinks that he is slipping. "No, he sent US here to work on this and that is what we are going to do, I mean look at what just happened to him. Come on, we've been in far worse situations, especially you Chris. I think that tomorrow the first thing for us to do is get out of here, get out of here without anyone knowing… (Bond speaks these next few words in a softer voice) I know that your mind is on Jane, I mean the two of you. I understand… you miss her, she is going through a lot right now, but look at it this way, and dad is back. Now they can try and outdo each other on morning trivia." Bond took one foot back and regained his stance looking to the floor then at Chris's face. Chris lightly breathes out and he opens his mouth, Bond looks to him for a response, but the air remains silent.

Bond takes another step backward; Chris remains locked for an instant. Another few silent seconds pass then they each go to their bedroom doors, turning the knobs at the same time. Soft words come from Chris, "You're right. Good night." He then goes inside his room and closes the door, Bond stands with his hand still in the unopened door, then pauses and breathes out, he replies, "I love you brother." He starts to take off his clothes for the night and then stops wearing only his pants, then sits sideways on the corner of the bed, holding his cell phone. "This has always been vital, but right now, I'm turning it off and locking the code." Now finished from the bathroom, he pulls the side covers from the bed and gets in adjusting his body to just the right place to fall asleep, he says to himself, "I hope this new guy will work out." He breathes out a heavy sigh, and then turns off the light, praying for a much-needed sleep.

Chris wipes a silent tear that falls on the right side of his face. He lay down with his head on two pillows, then reaches to another side of the empty bed. He moves his hand to feel only the bed covers. "I miss you; I miss you so much. I haven't felt well lately and I don't know if it is the absence of you in my life or something else. Sometimes dizziness plays with me, maybe just maybe it is…Jane, I miss you. You are my world, and our daughter.

Why? The only thing that I can do now is sleep." He turns his head to the side on the pillow looking to the empty side of the bed. "I doubt that sleep will come easy."

# Chapter 15

VINCENT SAT AT the end spot on the dining table at the estate, he was back to his usual routine of reading the newspaper and drinking aromatic coffee. Jane walked in quietly and sat down, then reached for the coffee pot and poured herself a cup. She looked to the end spot on the table where she could only see the newspaper, thinking that it was Bond, she said nothing. She made noise breathing in then looked at the unmoved newspaper. She took another sip of coffee then clanked it against the saucer placing it back down on the table. Still, no movement came from the paper. She was more than starting to feel annoyed. Finding no other option of anything to do she reached for biscotti from the middle of the table. Instead of dipping it in the coffee as she usually does, she clanked it against the side of the cup, making further noise. Still, the newspaper did not move.

She reached into her mind for anything to do without having to physically talk out loud. She breathed out loudly further annoyed, then proceeded to swallow another sip of coffee. At just that moment when her mouth was full of this liquid, the paper dropped, and Vincent smiled to her. "I am back, tell me, is there something wrong?" She looked into his face then could not contain the coffee in her mouth- it started to fly out, she instantly raised her napkin to her face to shield the liquid from flying out.

She then dropped open-mouthed, opened her eyes wide and then blinked. "You are back!"

He passes her a circular plate of fresh fruit; she nods her head to him and takes an orange. She now shows joy instead of grief over her body and smiles at him. He takes more coffee and nods in return. She starts to peel his orange, and then blinks as some of the juice hit her face. He places the folded newspaper on the table to the side of him. She waits for him to say something, and not hearing anything she then springs forth in conversation. "What was the first team to win the Super bowl?" She smirks then squiggles in her chair, thinking that she had him. He licks his lips, and then leans back in the chair showing a bit of confusion. She smirks even wider. "That would be Bart Star plays for the Green Bay Packers; he won the following year as well." She dropped her hands to her lap in defeat and expelled a sigh. He then leans forward looking directly at her and asks, "What about the third one?"

She rises back up her body in the chair and holds the coffee cup tighter. "That would be the handsome Joe Namath." He nods his head to her then asks, "But what team did he play for?" She takes a moment then says, "New York." "Ah, but New York who? There are two times that play for New York."

She looked bewildered, then grabs hold of her orange gets up and leaves the table almost running from it. "I'll find out." He takes a deep breath in and then exhumes, "Things are returning to normal around here." He takes another sip of coffee then dips a biscotti in it, takes a bite chew swallows, and laughs. "I'm feeling a lot better."

# Chapter 16

HOURS PASSED SINCE they turned in for the night in Las Vegas. Troy had fallen asleep with an open book over his body, Bond had finally stopped searching for that perfect spot and was now snoring. But Chris was still fighting with his body. He lay down under the sheets with his eyes closed and body weak, he was physically fighting in his mind, a dream, a dream of the past. He could see himself running down an alley of a foreign country, he could hear bullets bombing the air surrounding his body; he contracted his shoulders, feeling the unnerving trauma of the run, his heartbeat faster at the sound of each bullet. His mind races, will I make it? He clenches himself over the sheets sweating profusely; I am in trouble, death is chasing me.

He fights with the bed the sheets sweating gasping for air, then turns over raises his upper body out of bed, and widens his eyes traumatized expressing the most panicked fear imaginable. He breathes out then clenches his fingers. His eyes tear, he lifts his neck to the ceiling, then lowers it behind him. In an outburst, he cries out, "What am I doing? Where am I?" he moves out to the side of the bed and sits there with his feet on the floor. "What is happening? What is going on?" he tries to stand, but then falls back down to the bed. "I can't do this, why, why?" he tries softly breathing and deeply to calm his racing heart that he can feel pound at the back of his neck. He lifts his hand to his forehead presses in then moves it stopping right over his eyebrow.

He tries with all his might and feels his knees gave way bending to the floor; he takes his open hand to the top of the bed and catches himself. "Why now, after all these years, this isn't happening, it can't happen. I am dreaming, that has to be it, a living nightmare of a dream. I need help, but the timing, I can't, I have to be strong. I have a family." He stands to look out to the view thinking the view of the evening would relax him. But all that he can see is solemn darkness, the sheltering of the windows. He opens his mouth, then moves his tortured physical being back to the bed and lays there looking void. This is my world.

The sun had just risen over the Vegas Valley; Bond is already up and dressed pacing the floor of the front of the house. "It should be ready now." He eagerly walks to the kitchen and sees the last drop falling into the coffee pot. He is already holding a cup waiting to capture it. With the coffee poured just to the right mark to pour some cream in he turns from the refrigerator and drops it to just the right spot before tipping out of the cup. He still very carefully takes it to his mouth and takes a sip followed by two more.

"It's good, but the ironic thing is I can't start the day without it. And Starbuck's loves to hear that from everybody." He picks up a granola bar, then places it back down on the counter and makes a sour face. "I can't eat now."

"Timing is getting crucial; the day hasn't even started yet- good thing that I turned out making plans for this morning last night." Troy enters the kitchen, Bond offers him coffee, he declines it and takes a glass bottle from the refrigerator instead. While opening it, he tells Bond that he never developed a taste for coffee, but sometimes he drinks tea. Bond didn't verbally respond; he just nodded his head in response. Troy asked Bond where Chris was. Bond moved his head, looking around the room, and then he thought it was very odd that Chris wasn't there as he was usually the first one up and already sweating from working out in some fashion. He put his coffee cup on the kitchen counter, and then left for the bedroom to look for him.

Bond lightly knocked on Chris's door; he waited for never-ending minutes, no response. Bond thought with all planned for that morning he has to be already ready. He then thought, maybe he is still in the shower. He decided to go in and check. Much to his surprise, Chris lay still in bed. fear ravished Bond's mind, is he alright? He ran to the bed and lifted his wrist checking for a pulse, there was one. He then thought, why didn't he open his eyes and why isn't he up? He reached down to touch him tapping his body, then said in a regular to him, "Chris, Chris, come on, it is morning." The sheets started to move, there was a response. He still hadn't opened his eyes though.

Bond saw no other option but to keep shaking him and calling his name. Grumbling was then heard; this was a relief to Bond to hear. "Are you alright?" Chris mumbled some more then rose up from the bed. It looked to Bond that Chris had a bit too much to drink the night before. "Are you drunk?" Chris turned his head from side to side making a sour face. "No, I am not drunk. It just did not feel well last night and it took me a long time to fall asleep." "It looks like you just did. Is there a problem?" Chris then moved his hands up and down his bent thighs, and yawned, "No, there is no problem, give me twenty minutes and I'll be right out there." Bond left to the door then stopped while it was still open. "Pack all of your stuff; we are moving out, today." Chris thought, moving, they just got there, then he remembered the previous night, he said nothing in response so he just went to the bathroom and closed that door. Once Bond saw this, he returned to the kitchen.

Troy had already packed or never unpacked his bags, they were to the side of the rear door of the house. Bond noted him while he reached for his cup, and then took a sip. "Jeez, it is cold." He dumps it in the sink, and then refills his cup, "Well, what did I expect?" A buzzer rings, he goes to the side control panel where the alarm box is, he presses a button, then listens, "Okay, drive up." He then presses a button to release the front gate. He then goes to the front door and fights the implies to open it wide, not knowing what or who is leering in the hillside. Now seeing the truck approach, then park, he gets a call on a cell phone that everything is alright. He then reaches for the doorknob, but still fights with his hesitation to open it. He looks to the air above him, and then grabs hold of the gold necklace he is wearing then looks forward and goes out to the truck.

He talks with one of the three workers; they seem to agree with it, then they all nod their heads. He goes back inside the open door but still watching them. All of a sudden, a voice from behind him speaks, "Carpet cleaners?" It was Chris holding a cup of coffee. "You're up already?" Chris takes another swallow and then replies, "And packed." "That must have been some shower." The carpet cleaning machines have been brought inside and the three of the workers as well. Chris looks puzzled to Bond, and then Bond leads him to his bedroom to explain the needed course of action. Troy was already there. "Why is he wearing a carpet cleaning uniform?" Bond then replied, "We all are and hands Chris a uniform."

An hour or so later, the workers get back in the truck and leave, stopping only to wait for the front gate to open for them to leave. The truck then gets on the freeway and heads north on the 95. In the back of the truck, Bond changes out of the work uniform and tells Chris to as well. Chris then smirks, "You are going to take father's place that was a good one." Bond says thanks and then looks to Troy and asks him, "how much longer?" Troy tells him that it is the next exit then ten or fifteen minutes more.

Exiting the freeway, turning to the right, they look out the side window and see it is an average commercial street of any city: At Burger King, a Woolworth, a gas station, and a grocery store. He then turns onto a busier three-lane street in each direction. Then after passing an auto part store, the country seems to momentarily take over for a brief spell. They look out to the now quietness of a hustling busy city, the next thing is a turn into a small courtyard with just four homes. The single-story home in the middle of the court has a large side driveway that goes even further back than the house. They stop there. The truck is rather hidden from view.

They all get out, then stretch their tired bodies. Chris looks up to the sky and watches a flying bird go by, "I like this." Bond responds, "The house and the bedrooms here are nothing like what you had, so don't get too happy." "Yes, it is work." Two large German Shepherds run parking at the cyclone fence surrounding the house and guest casita, three other sidewalls of the house are stone, this is the only exception. Bond opens the conversation between dog barks. "And what are we supposed to do about that or these?" he looks to Troy, who goes right up to the fence; the dogs wag their tails and jump on the fence, seems happy. "What, how?" Bond looks puzzled; Chris just stands silent and watches.

"Oh, I have met these two before, you see the owner, she is away on a short vacation and her son is staying with some friends of his in town. I have come here before to stake this place out and it seemed to be just what we are looking for the short time and we'll be using it." Bond tilted his head and gave a half-smile. Chris sprang into verse, "And what about my car?" "Oh, in talking with your dad, he said that something so ostentatious should be out of view for now. He has arranged for this to be picked up and two other cars brought here for you." Bond showed anger all through his body as he opened his speech in a very angry tone. "I just made these plans last night and carried them through this morning, how would he ever know or find out?!" Chris steps to the gate, "I texted him." Bond stands frozen with his mouth open.

They go inside the house and scope out their room. Bond has no idea on the room he wants, there are only two bedrooms and an office and all of them have windows." It seems that I can't escape this dilemma." Chris walks by him in the hall carrying his suitcase. "Okay, I'll take the Master." He goes in then shuts the door. Bond goes inside the other room. "I guess that this was set up for kids, one sleep under the bed on the floor and the other has to climb this short ladder to get to the bed, and he goes inside and closes the door..., the window is right there, in front of the house. Oh, boy." He goes inside and closes the door, "I hope that we don't have to stay here long."

They then met back up at the dining table to the side of a small kitchen. A small truck comes and stops at the front of the house. The two brothers' look worried, Troy tells them that this is okay; one of them will get out and pick up the carpet cleaning truck. They watch this happen from the backyard. The dogs seemed to have made peace with them. Bond is happy about this but shows no expression. Chris reached down and pets the top of the larger dogs' heads. It nudged up to the side of him and wanted more. He gave it one more pet then reached down for a tennis ball and threw it in this large backyard ¾ of an acre. "That pool over there (he points to a gated pool) looks inviting." Troy replies, "let's get everything taken care of before we think about that."

# Chapter 17

A BLACK STRETCH LIMO enters the estate in Hawaii. Vincent steps outside the front door under the portico to meet it. The driver gets out, and then opens the side door in the back. A tall man gets out, Vincent instantly recognizes who it is. He smiles, and then takes four steps forward. The man stands straight holding a walking cane as he slowly moves toward Vincent. The driver leaves in the limo. Standing in front of the house with the door open the two embraces and hug, then stand back from each other and smile, and then Vincent waves his hand forward for them to proceed into the house. Now inside Jonathan drops his suitcase to the floor. "It is good to see you, you gave us quite a scare. Let's get a drink." Jonathan walks inside the living room. "I would take you up on that, but with the current medication that I am on, no drinks allowed."

Vincent pours them each a glass of still iced water, then hands one to Jonathan sitting on the couch. Then he sits on the chair to the side of the couch. They both take a sip and smile at each other. "Has a doctor given you any plans for your recovery?" Jonathan looks into the glass then pauses. "No, I have only seen the doctor that went to treat me at the house." Vincent nods, still wondering if he was going to hear more or if he should take over the conversation. "I am sure that you know everything here on this island, your home that you could tell me about one." Vincent then relaxes then straightens himself back up sitting straight back in the chair. "Yes, yes,

I will surely get one for you. Being the time now, it'll have to wait until tomorrow." Jonathan snickers, "Tomorrow or the next day will be fine. I am not going anywhere."

They continue laughing; telling stories of yesterday, then go to the dining room as the servant brought them there. The dinner was fried chicken, mashed potatoes and gravy, and snow peas. Jonathan looked to this full plate, and then smiled at Vincent. "Comfort food, at it's very best. Thank you." finished with the wonderful dinner, Jonathan slides his chair back making himself more comfortable. Seeing this, Vincent at first worries then relaxes as Jonathan told him that he was just making himself comfortable. Vincent relaxed hearing this.

The servant then brings out an apple pie, places it into two plates and pie server to the middle of the table then places a small pot of coffee in the middle of the table. Vincent asks Jonathan if he would like some pie. Jonathan declines but told him that he would love the coffee. Vincent pours the coffee, then they each take their cups back to the living room and resume the conversation. Vincent then asks him if he remembered anything of what he found out in Las Vegas. Jonathan clicks his spoon in the cup, twirling it then looks blankly at the cup, the ceiling then to the face of Vincent.

He breathes out and apologizes, "I had everything that I found out on the tablet and the tablet was in the condo. I do not know if it is still there or not. The doctor told me that from what did happen to me, there may be a short or full-term memory loss of the event that led up to what happened to me. It may come back. Vincent, you know me, I am thorough." He stops and takes a sip. Then he continues to look down at the cup instead of looking Vincent in the eyes, as he is embarrassed at what did happen to him. "I do remember though, that I had had the plan." Vincent looks straight to him at first showing a look of concern then hardens his facial expression. "Plan, what plan? Is this from the gang that we are trying to stop? This isn't identity theft; it is something larger than that.

Do you remember anything to do with medical?" "That is just it, Vincent, I know that I know, I just cannot remember."

Jonathan looks out to the beach, his eyes lock in that direction away from the view of Vincent. Vincent more than picks up on this. "It has been a long day for you. Can you make it up the stairs? I'll send for someone to help you." Before Jonathan could even form the words to reply to him a guard was already there to help him. "Thank you, Vincent; it will be a new day tomorrow." Watching him leave, Vincent wondered at the meaning of that remark. He then wondered about the absence of Jane, surely she must have heard something or she was hungry for dinner, where was she? He sat back in the chair thinking of all current situations and then paused as something was not right. The guard wasn't there; he could feel the presence of another entity in the room. He swallowed his heart and looked for this presence, then relaxed his composure and smiled at her. It was Jane. She came no further to him remaining at the edge of the room. "Joe Namath played for the New York Jets, and he finished with the l.A. rams. He was elected to the hall of fame and named MVP in 1968." She smiled at him, exhuming the look of "ha, ha". Vincent let out a deep breath of air, feeling very comfortable. "Here is another one for you, what quarterback has won the most Super Bowl's?" She smiled widely at him. He remained quiet. "That is easy, Mr. Tom Brady- six of them…so far. I feel like a hot dog." She left for the kitchen.

A deep cough overwhelmed him; he began to worry, could it be a sign of the virus? I am abiding by the shelter in place; hopefully it is just a cough and nothing more. Maybe some music to calm me, taking the remote off of the coffee table, he pressed it, and then the room was filled with the sounds of a fifth of Beethoven, an utter classic, he thought. He sat there for a few more minutes then feeling disturbed that he wasn't doing anything. He decided to go to the kitchen and check on Jane.

The room was a bit dark and the overhead ceiling light was not on, only the light from the stove was on. He noticed this thought it a bit odd, but said nothing. She was sitting at the table holding a half-eaten hot dog and all of a sudden, she seemed lifeless so to say. He observed her and being that he stood directly to the side of her, surely, she had to have noticed him. It was like a witch just placed a spell on her, some transferred from overwhelming happiness to despair and grief. He decided to sit and good thing that he did, in a violent course of motion, she hurled herself from the chair, threw down the unfinished hot dog, and ran way both screaming and crying.

Vincent sat there looking grief-stricken himself. With deep despair, he envisioned the face of his departed wife. He bit his lips closed his eyes and replied, "This currently is a sad house, it is a sad world right now." He rose up out of the chair and headed to his bedroom.

# Chapter 18

THE MEN IN Vegas were barbequing at the backyard of the house they are staying, Chris played ball with the dogs. Barking and tail wags were a nice welcome sight. Troy was at the BBQ; Bond sat at the patio table smiling viewing everything. Troy brought a plate of food to the table. Chris viewed him doing this. Now they all sat there putting relish, mustard, and catsup on their hot dogs. The two dogs lay down at each side of Chris and looked up to him waiting for any handout. Troy saw this, and then told him that he could put them inside so they wouldn't bother him while eating. Chris said, "No, it was okay."

"This is nice. I can even see some of the valley's hills here. The only thing missing is…" They all picked up on these words from Bond. Troy looked to their lost faces, and then said, "I can get us women, and all it takes is one call." Both Bond and Chris replied at the same time, "No." Troy then flapped his hands forward, "Okay then, I didn't mean anything, and it is just what I, never mind." Bond quietly whispered out the name Laurie. Chris asked him,

"Who is Laurie?" "Just someone that I, I used to know." Chris now knew to leave this alone.

Now done with dinner, Chris went back inside the house to the kitchen and came out with three oranges juggling them, then threw one to each man then sat and started peeling his. Bond said, "So tomorrow, we will each go our ways?" Chris jumped in, "It is too soon for Troy (he pointed his body toward Troy) to go there, I think that we should wait at least a day maybe two for you to pop up." "But suppose he gets someone else?" "Think about it, it is not a job that you are going to find on Indeed or Monster."

"We have to give him time to miss that person being there. He has got a problem." "More than just one problem." They all laugh. "Betting, the forms are always over the desk, and he does tend to 'run' off for undisclosed periods. He needs someone to be there to cover for him."

"It just all needs to be done very carefully," Troy says that he has a pull at a casino. "No, we can't name names and right now with this pandemic, casinos are closed. We have to find out where he is going, this is something illegal. A true gambler can never be without. There are or will be placed to do this, we just have to find out where." "This makes it all the harder, I mean it is not like I can go to the back of the betting line at the Westgate, and just watch him." "The Westgate?" "It is one of the premier sports gambling casinos in this town." "You mean city." "That too." later that evening Chris goes for a swim in the backyard pool, Bond still is not at ease enough to do this. He watches him and the surroundings very closely while he is in the pool. Troy has been practicing some Karate moves on the grass, the dogs chew bones. Bond views it all and thinks of how relaxed everything is which makes him worry more. The night sky has approached, he looks up then calls them all in. Chris towels off and the larger dog runs to him and is right under his hand walking inside the house. He puts both of the dogs then closes the door. He then comments that he is not tired enough to go to bed right now, Troy says the same. Bond has no comment.

Chris showers and changes into some sweats, Troy scours the kitchen, and then made some popcorn; Bond enters the new password to his laptop and checks on it. They all make themselves comfortable at the TV; Bond still gets up and views the small 6-inch side window of the front door. Troy holds the remote. He stops on a James Bond movie that is just starting. Chris nods his head to it, Bond sits down showing no emotion, and they all view it with the comfort of popcorn.

With the movie over and all more relaxed, they turn in. Troy goes to the outside casita. Chris goes to the master bedroom and Bond to the smaller side room where he has to climb a small ladder to get to the top of the raised bed. To the direct side of the bed is a window. The shutters are drawn, only darkness remains, but he can still find no comfort. He climbs out of the bed and looks directly at the floor. That doesn't seem like a comfortable option. He then leaves the bedroom and goes to the living room couch, then sees the windows on each side of the TV and the front door and glass doors to open to the backyard. On the other side of the house he finds only the garage, opening it he sees an empty garage and a side window but to the side of it a folded cot. He brings that back in the house then sets it open in the hallway, covers him with a blanket and pillow, and turns in for the night, surprisingly falling instantly to sleep.

The following morning Chris left the master bedroom yawning and had nothing but the taste of coffee on his mind. He came to a sudden stop feeling the cot. He looked down opening his eyes from the yawn and saw his brother still asleep on the cot in the middle of the hallway. He looked down at him surprised that his presence did not wake him. "Did you fight last night and she threw you out?" he opened his eyes with a questioning look, "What, where?" he then took his arm to his face moaned and got up.

Then he folded the cot, "I, Uhm" "I know you don't like windows. I am going to get breakfast started, I advise you to go clean up."

Both Chris and Troy were eating at the kitchen table. Bond came in and looked at them at the table, then went back to the kitchen counter and poured himself a cup of coffee. The two were eating scrambled eggs with cinnamon toast that Chris made. Bond reached over for the half and a half, and then stirred his coffee. He was then handed a plate. The dogs barked. He commented while holding up a fork of food to his mouth, "Do they need to be fed?" Troy commented back, "I already fed them and walked them." He continued to eat. He stopped eating halfway through his meal. Seeing this, Chris asked him if there was something wrong. "It is just that I am used to eating outside in the morning." Chris replied, "Go ahead" and moved his arm in the direction of the door. Bond got up holding his plate and coffee, Troy opened the door for him. They both watched him go outside then place his food and coffee on the table and sit down. Both of the dogs were happy and the smaller one brought him a ball to throw for them. In five minutes, he was back inside the house. "It is just too damn hot out there, and it is only 8:30 in the morning." Troy laughed, "It's Vegas."

The noise of car engines led them to the front of the house, Chris opened the front door. A man stepped toward him with a pad and he signed for them and was handed the keys. Bond looked to him then said, "When did you take over?" Chris said nothing, only handed Bond a set of keys. He then walked further out the door to see them, and one was a beautiful shiny white Mustang convertible and the other is a four-door sedan of no distention. Chris went back in the house, "The Mustang is mine." Bond looked to the sedan, the keys then Chris, "figures."

They spent the next two days getting accustomed to the Vegas area and the roads and freeways, where certain things were to be found and where certain areas were to avoid. On the third day, Troy went to the storage facility. Larry was there in the office expressing a view that he just lost everything, and racing forms were at the side end of the counter.

He went to the office and talked of the day, said "hello" the average daily insignificant jargon. Larry never even lifted his head from the view of the counter looking very lost in all respects. Troy then stood nervous; Larry picked up on this then viewed him still only with his head halfway up to view him straight-faced. Troy said nothing. Larry responded, "Do you have a problem or something? What are you looking for?" responding physically very timidly, "A job." This brought a small smile to Larry's face. In the next hour, Troy was driving the Cushman scooter around the grounds and had keys to everything and the toolbox in the back of the scooter. He even wore an employee jacket and hat. He was happy that this was so easy, but this also meant to be more on the lookout for everything and everybody. He played with a slight Southern accent and gave the appearance that nothing more than the 6th-grade education. He used a black paste to make it seem that a few teeth were missing. He always was very polite in every aspect.

He did only what was asked of him and nothing more. Mentally, he took everything in as far as where things were, the people that came in and out, he noticed the large trucks that went to that one particular storage building and paid it special attention. If there were even a very brief time when he had no specific thing to do, he drove back to the office and swept in the front of it and all around every side of it. He saw Larry watch him do this, but paid no attention to him, making him very secure that he hired a dumb person who just wanted to work without question.

# Chapter 19

CHRIS DROVE AROUND the city and made stops at various places like the front of casinos, especially making him look like a typical tourist. On occasion he did drive off the strip to the residential streets, taking in the neighborhoods. One stop that he made in particular: something about it caught his attention. He was stopped at a gas station with a large walk-in market. After he finished pumping the gas he parked to the side of the building and went in, covering his face with the mask as it was now required in almost every place. Inside the small market, with refrigerator walls of soft drink beers and aisles of chips, snacks, and toiletries. He lowered his dark glasses to get used to the light change of bright store lights, and then pushed them back up. He grabbed a large can of iced tea and a small bag of cashews. He paid the Oriental male clerk that was on his cell phone. Chris more than thought that he didn't even look at him just what Chris put them on the counter. The only time that they made the briefest contact was when he put his change on the counter.

Back to his car at the side of the building, he opened the can of iced tea and took a few sips then opened the bag of nuts. The top of the wrapper fell to the ground. He set the can down and tried to pick up the wrapper, just as he was about to grab it the wind blew it slightly away, this happened two more times. He was about to lose it and give up, then he thought that he was not going to let the wrapper win. As he stood up, he was much closer to the building at the side and the back of the convenience store gas station.

Something about it, the paint peeling from the dull white and brown walls or the heavy door that had a faded sign above the doorway. What was it? He didn't want to make himself known of what he was doing. He took two more steps in front of him then poured of nuts in his hand and took them into his mouth as he saw it was the sign of a bar, "lucky Bar". Bars and restaurants were now closed by state order for the virus. But seeing the few cars in the small parking lot in front of it, it appeared to still be doing business. He then thought of the time and of how he'd better get out of there. He went back to his car with the soda and nuts then drove away.

# Chapter 20

BOND DROVE THROUGH the part of Vegas that was the Summerlin district on the west side of the city. Parts of Summerlin were known for their more expensive housing tracts. Looking to his right, he saw a large building that reminded him of Italy in the architecture, hence the name Tivoli Village. It appeared in offices and various shops. The first thing in his mind was an expensive tourist trap. He drove into a small complex in-between Tivoli and a large target shopping center. "Okay a large, liquor wine store, a hair salon, a Panera, and restaurants that do not open until dinner and right now will not open. This area was very busy and in just slowing down to wait for traffic, he either got honked at or driven by. He quickly decided to leave and went to Tivoli instead. To his surprise, he could see a few people walking with paper coffee cups. He parked and then look for the location of this store where he could get a coffee.

He put his dark glasses on as the sun was now shining bright there. He found the spot; it was an Italian bakery that served coffee specialties. Instead of having his usual coffee with half and half, he opted for a non-fat latte, and the croissants looked irresistible, he ordered one of those heated. Even in the extremely small space there, the few tables and chairs were strapped down; the only option was to go outside. There were no tables or chairs there either. He walked back to his car, then saw a cement post against the parking lot where he could set his coffee and croissant to eat it. In just minutes in doing this, he saw that he was not alone doing this.

To his right, there were four other posts and they were all being used by patrons doing the same as him.

The croissant was better than he expected it to be. Warm flaky in just biting into it, flakes flew off. The woman standing to the right side of him turned her head toward him, and then retracted it back from the blaring glare of the sun. Her scent was nice as a soft spicy flower, it was familiar. He smiled at her wanting to see more and maybe get her name. He saw that she was finished with her coffee and pastry-he had better do something fast. He was for that moment dumbstruck for what to say, but he couldn't let her get away. He panicked as he saw her leave, in trying to grab his coffee and croissant at the same time, he spilled some on his shirt. He felt the warm liquid on his skin, thankfully it didn't burn but he more than felt it. He grabbed a Kleenex out of his pant pocket and started blotting it dry. He didn't even notice that during the time that he was doing this, she walked right up to him.

"I can see why you spilled it; it is not as good as mine." He looked to this woman feeling embarrassed then when he saw who it was, he was further embarrassed and happy at the same time. He widened his eyes and almost dropped what he was holding. "I left you speechless?" he smiled more but said nothing. She looked to him, and then started to leave not hearing anything from him. He reached for her and place his hand on her shoulder. "Come on, it is such a shock on seeing you again, it is great." They started receiving unpleasant looks from other people there. "Masks," They then put their face masks back on and went to his car. He opened the passenger door and she got in. Once he was inside, they each took off their face masks. "A four-door Nissan, you have come down on what you drive." Again, feeling embarrassed he told her that it was just for the time that he was there. "Strange time to be taking a vacation." "Something to do with business. I should only be here for a short time, then I'll be back on the island." She nodded but did not seem to be that happy with his explanation. "What brought you here?" She leaned back breathed out then started answering his question.

"With the virus outbreak, I had to close. Jobs everywhere have become scarce. I have a cousin who works for the city here and she found me a job. I didn't want to leave the island, but I am not Donald Trump. Financially, I had to leave. I do miss lady very much though; I'll tell you that." He remembered lady is her dog. He closed his lips bit down and nodded his head. "She was a good dog; I mean is a good dog. What did you do with her?" he was nervous in asking this as he was afraid the answer was going to shelter. "I had a customer that she knew a little, and she said that she would take care of her. Of course, my long-term goal is to get back there." He nodded his head.

"You are lucky that you have a cousin here." She nodded. "And you here, now, is this part of spy school 101?" he laughed, "let's just say that it is for now, anyway." The next few moments were silent; they could each tell that the other wanted to say something more. She looked forward out the front window, "There is my cousin now, she is waving. I don't know if she sees me here or not but I had better go." He quickly wrote down his cell number on the back of the coffee receipt and gave it to her. She put it in her purse. He could tell that she wanted to say or do something more, it was like she stalled with her hand on the open-door handle. She kissed the side of his cheek ever so lightly, and then left the car. He watched every move that she made in getting to her cousin then walked away from his view. He smiled, feeling much better; he waited a minute, and then left the parking lot.

# Chapter 21

L ARGE TRUCKS CAME and went all through the day at the storage facility. Troy noticed it and it was always that one building. At one time when it was unloading at the open storage doors to the building, he saw two men hurriedly pushing a silver cart that stood two and a half feet tall and 18 inches wide. They had just dropped it off or left it there and they were already leaving. Troy hides behind the side corner of the neighboring building. He didn't want to be seen. But why should there be a problem if he was seen, he worked there. After they left, he went back to Cushman then drove away to the garage, then went to the counter where he kept needing tools and supplies then took his water bottle, opened it and had a drink. All through this, he thought of why the hurry? It was like they didn't want to be seen. He knew that he couldn't ask Larry anything about it. Larry had to know or was he that much dazed to life?

Standing outside of the office he saw Larry exit the building and go to his truck. It wasn't until he was in his truck and driving away that he stops the truck and lower the window, and yelled out, "I am leaving, don't know when I'll be back, you stay here and take care of the place." He then hit the accelerator on the gas and almost hit the gate driving out in a hurry. Troy counted down a minute, then went into the office. Building "B" is where all this is happening. He opened the four-drawer file cabinet surprised to still see one as everything today was on the computer. More safety he thought. No one could access this information from afar, only here.

With the third drawer open, there it was right in the middle of the files, Phoenix Corporation. He stopped hearing the bell of the front door open. He casually pushed the drawer closed. In turn to see who this was, he breathed a sigh of relief seeing an older couple, who simply came in to pay their monthly bill. He took their check, then gave them a receipt and watched them leave. He again very carefully pulled out the file and noticed that on each of the four sides of it was a paper clip. He wondered why this was for safety so that nothing would fall out, but why on each side when even just one would do the job. Then he deduced, trap. He left it alone and closed the file cabinet. The next few hours there proved exhausting.

He even went as much as to view the operating expenses.

When he first saw it, he thought that there had to be something wrong.

The electric bill on this place revealed Caesar's Palace. "Why so high?"

A woman then came in and explained her trouble getting the lock off her locker. He locked the office, put up the sign on the door and drove off to her problem. Then a man's dog got out of his truck and he found that he spent well over an hour trying to track down this dog and safely get it back to the man. Other various things happened, one right after another. A kid playing with the water hose at the side of the building and leaving it out with the water turned on full force. Before he knew it, it was closing time. And Larry hadn't returned yet. The gates were going to go on alarm very soon. This was new, since the ordeal with Chris. The police made sure that an alarm was put in.

He contemplated whether to get out of there before the alarm did set or if he should stay there and have a closer look through everything. He then thought that this was more of the job that one of the brothers should do and not him. He opted for the safer choice and got out of there in time. He'd just report back to the brothers of his findings.

Leaving the locked alarmed gate, he turned left from the driveway, and then left at the first stop three blocks down. Instead of getting in the far-right lane to enter the freeway, he got in the far-left lane and then saw it was a turn lane that went directly to the hospital. Not liking the idea of visiting a hospital, he made a U-turn there instead of left to go the hospital parking lot. The only other building to the side was a rest home. After seeing this, he went back to enter the freeway to go home.

The cars of each of the brothers were there. But there was something different about the front of this home now. He parked at the long dirt driveway at the side of the house, and then went inside; both Bond and Chris were there. They were watching the evening news. It was more news on the pandemic and stating of a large number of recorded cases in New York City and New Orleans was reported to be the current epicenter of the virus. Las Vegas currently had 100 reported cases and it was getting worse all over. Then a reminder aired, to always wash your hands, cover your face, and stay home. Hearing that Troy was silent, then went to the kitchen sink and thoroughly washed his hands and face, then threw away the paper towel that he used to dry himself. Bond turned the TV off and they went to the kitchen. Chris then took a basket of el Pollo loco from the oven. They all sat down and helped themselves to this meal.

Bond started the conversation. "The day was nice heat-wise anyway, only 88, today." They shook their heads in agreement. Troy asked, "Do we say what we learned today during or wait until after we eat?" Between bites, while chewing Chris said, "That depends." "Depends on what?" Chris swallows, "If it is good news or bad news." "Good," They all stop and give their full attention to Troy. He tells them what he found in the storage facility that day. Bond looks to Chris and asks him, "Should we go there now to uncover the rest of this information?" Chris takes another serving of coleslaw then simply replies, "No."

Bond then remains silent and thinks I am the boss, but he did ask him. "Not meaning to change the subject but…why is there a panel truck parked in front of the house?" "That is so Bond can sleep." Troy looked to both of them for further explanation. Passing seconds went by then the dogs barked. "I have been fired at when I was sleeping on a bed one time, and that was all it took. I do not like and cannot have windows in my bedroom." "Were you hit?" he did not respond to the question; Chris made a facial expression to leave that question alone. He finished up then went outside to the dogs.

Bond then told Chris that he is going to be playing the doctor's role again. Chris reminded him that was against the law. He agreed, "I will only be playing doctor doing no more than talk to patients and put in an appearance." "Yes, and you do have that information in your head from when you took that health class in college, you always remind me." Bond was put back by this and said nothing to answer him. "Well, what is going to do dear brother?" At that point Bond knew what he wanted to say, but he knew that he had better not, "Anything that you want." Chris was taken aback, "What do you mean by that?" he didn't receive an answer but knew better than to push the situation.

After the table was cleaned off and Bond looked at him. "Lucky bar, it seems that we have both seen it. Is this for a reason?" "Do you think that maybe this is where Larry goes?" "We need to find out what's going on there." "Both Troy and I will be recognized by Larry, it seems that this will be your job." Chris throws the kitchen towel to Bond and he catches it right as he finished this sentence.

# Chapter 22

INSIDE THE VALLEY Views hospital, busy nurses', doctors'; orderlies', patients, people waiting and crying to be seen. Over the loudspeaker: "Dr. Lowe is paging. Dr. Lowe, emergency room stat." Bond pushes against swinging doors leading to the back of the hospital; patients on gurneys wave their hands in the air and cry to him. He lunges forward in each step making it seem like an utter emergency to get where he needs to go, but really to avoid the responsibility of any kind.

Surgeries were performed on the basement floor. No public entrance was in the basement for people to enter. The wide hallways were barren of people. Only when the elevator doors opened and bodies on gurneys were pushed out then taken into O.r.'s. Or bodies being taken out in quick transit to get to recovery or pushed slowly into the morgue. A nurse followed one being later. She looked at Bond inquisitively, "Do you need to get somewhere? Nobody just stands in this hallway." He showed fear over his body, "I am in training. I am to view, a watch." She is walking further away from him following the cart. "You better be quick, that is O.r. 7, for the heart transplant." He nodded his head, then stopped in front of O.r.7, and reviewed in from the oval top window. An assistant dressed in full surgery attire went to the window. He spoke to the window, "You had better be sterile and put on your mask before you come in here."

Bond knew that he wasn't sterile; he just continued to view this operation from behind the glass. He saw the operating surgeon take a brief look at him and then say something to the attendant at the side of him. In the silence, he could even hear to talk through the door. They are saying that I am new, and this is probably scaring me, is a lot different from just reading about it in a textbook. It is getting used to the blood and the inner-workings, organs of the body. He felt nauseous. The back wall of the operating room was a large steel rectangular door. The surgeon had already cut the patient open. This made Bond swallow hard and blink his eyes. A code was punched in the side of this metal frame and it opened, a nurse immediately went to it and brought it to the side of the surgeon. Bond could not believe what he saw and he could barely stomach it.

It was a live beating heart encased in blood. The patient's heart was then skillfully removed and the new beating heart from the steel box was transferred to his body. The surgeon then worked more on it. Bond literally felt queasy, heavy, and light-headed. He stepped back nearly falling then collapsed on the floor. The noise of this was heard inside the operating room. The surgeon made a foul expression. Another nurse to the side of him replied that it was just an intern in training observing his first surgery. The surgeon replied get him out of there, and now.

The door was then opened by an assistant nurse, the hallway was empty. She nodded, and then the body was wheeled out and to the elevator to go to recovery. Bond laid against the wall of the main floor, a doctor then stopped at his feet and asked him what the problem was. Bond replied in a shaky voice, "Just everything. I can't believe what I have seen." "We can't have you like this, go home and get some rest; we do need you, but not like this." Bond tried getting up but just seemed destined to be on the floor. "Take your time but not too long, we can't have the patients see you like this." He then rolled himself up, took off the jacket and left it at the side of the registration counter on his way out.

Outside of the hospital in the parking lot at the very last row against the cyclone fence was Bond holding the front end of his car leaning over to the ground and throwing up. He moved his head up appearing to be crying with no tears. He balanced himself to stand tall, and then bent over again. Nothing more came out, but he felt that he wanted to release something, anything. He balanced his body against the car and made it to the door. He stopped there and looked at the fence, then made an expression, what do I do now? He lifted his body straight up in an instant, then reached for the keys from his pocket and opened the door. He sat down, adjusted, and fastened the seat belt then hurled his face to the side of the open door and threw up again. He moved back with his back against the seat and then he whispered the words, "It can't be, we are, they are playing God." He took his hands off of the steering wheel then placed them flat open on his legs. He looked to the view of the fence out the window.

He sat there a few more minutes staring into what he could not see. A security cart lowered its pace right behind Bond. Bond saw this in the rear-view mirror and thought I did not want to talk to anybody right now, especially here. He then turned the key and started the engine and put it in reverse slowly backing out. The security then drove away. "The only place I can go right now is home, home, is not here." He did return to the house in the court then went to the bedroom and closed the door. He didn't even hear the sound of the dogs barking in the backyard. He got in the bed and closed his eyes literally to life.

# Chapter 23

A LARGE TRUCK WITH the emblem Phoenix enterprises backed into the gated building. The gate closed right after it entered. It's parked in front of a garage door, the driver and the passenger then stopped and waited for the large garage door to open. It stopped just three feet from the top, it stayed parked still, unmoved, still waiting for it to again move and reach the top. It finally did and then it drove in, the gate instantly closed behind it.

The two men then jumped out, the man on the passenger door side kept his door open for two more men from the back to jump out. All doors were closed and they walked to the partially open door of the side office. The same three men from the ones that Bond saw at the liquor store were there. The men that departed the truck handed a clipboard of information to the boss there. They will be handed each a roll of money, then told to be back tomorrow at 10 a.m. They nodded their heads, some laughing and then climbed two flights of stairs and exited the building.

He leaned back, smiled, and told his guard that the heart transplant netted them $40,000 today. There were the operation expenses, but he is still coming out great. He took a sip from his can of Coors's light, and then asked his guard what was on the agenda for tomorrow; the guard looked at the computer printout. Two liver transfers and one kidney, easily 60K. "And the necessary people at the hospital know about this?" "All taken care of." He leaned back in the chair, then remarked, "It is a good thing for me that it is still illegal here… money." He left the still open unfinished can of beer on the side of the desk, and then climbed the stairs followed by his guard to leave the building for the day. There were two large vans in the parking lot, displaying the name Phoenix enterprises on the right side. They each got in a silver Mercedes Sprinter van then turned left from the warehouse district and headed further west to a tall apartment high-rise. It parked in the gated lot and then the two of them traveled the elevator to the 14th-floor penthouse.

# Chapter 24

CHRIS DROVE INTO the court where the house is, seeing the large panel van in front of where Bond's bedroom is. To the side of that his Nissan and straight down the drive was Troy's vehicle, he parked in the garage then entered the house, walking around the washing machine and into the dining room/kitchen area. Nobody was there. "Well, their cars are here but?" he went out to the backyard and saw Troy playing with the dogs. He smiled at them; the larger dog came running to him. Troy then threw a tennis ball to him; he caught it then threw it to the dogs.

Troy met up with him, and then waited for him to speak. "Where is my brother?" Troy lifted his shoulders, "I haven't seen him since I got here. I saw his car but not him. I got here a bit late, sorry I didn't plan on anything for dinner." Chris told him not to worry about it, and then left to check to see where his brother was. Standing outside his brother's current bedroom, he stopped with his head to the door listening for anything. Hearing nothing, he lightly knocked on the door, he heard nothing in response. He gently opened the door saying his brother's name. Inside the room, he saw his brother on the bed and his appearance. He briskly went to his side, saying his name once more.

There was still no-response, he lifted his brother's wrist and felt and timed the pulse. "You have to give me something-say something, what happened?" he lifted his upper body then found difficulty moving his legs to the side of the bed. Chris then helped him do that. "I've got to get out of here; I've been here too long." Chris helped him out in the room and to the kitchen, where they sat at the kitchen table. Chris then grabbed two bottles of water from the refrigerator and opened them giving one to Bond. He sat there lifeless, still saying nothing. Chris then said to him, "Drink, drink." After the stillness remained for seconds, he finally took a sip followed by three more.

"You look like you've seen a ghost." Bond then thought of what he truly did see and the close connection to what his brother just said to him. Chris then asked him if Troy should hear this too. Bond nodded his head, yes. He was called in. He came in then reached for some Milk Bones and threw them to the dogs then closed the door. Seeing Bond's expression, he was worried then sat down to listen. Bond then explained everything that he saw from the hospital visit. The other two men were speechless- Troy with his mouth open in reaction to the news. Chris tried desperately to relax his demeanor then took a swallow of water. "Father said that it was going to be something very important, and it will be the biggest that we had to deal with ever." Bond then spoke, "It is like we are going up against God." Chris replied, "These I know are not ethical, but think about it if it was your child, wouldn't you want it?" Solemnness then encased the room. Bond replied straight-faced, "Yes."

Troy then told them of what he encountered throughout the day. And ended with, "This is the biggest goldmine ever." They nodded their head and Bond responded looking to Chris, "Get me a beer." A Stella was instantly put in his hand. Dinner that night was a green salad and sandwiches as none of them really felt like cooking and Bond not to eat. They knew they should though.

Finished with dinner, Bond went to the backyard and played with the dogs throwing the ball to them from sitting on a chair. The heat of the day subsided a bit. He got up and went to the swimming pool, walking around it several times looking at the moving water. He looked at the house and saw that Chris had come outside, he called him over. Bond asked him if they could each just sit down. They sat at the outside table and said nothing, but seemed to gather strength in just being together.

"The plate of that van that you saw at the liquor store, well, it is registered to, Phoenix enterprises." "Kind of no surprise there." Chris was happy; his brother was talking again, "Phoenix, life from the ashes." "A bird that would burn itself on a funeral nest of herbs to rise again fresh and beautiful for another long life." Bond looked at Chris intently, then smiled at him, "You always have to one-up me, don't you?" "That's what I am here for."

"I'm going to turn in and I have a lot of things that I have to work on tomorrow." "What am I going to do?" "Number one, stay out of the hospital," Bond smiled then lifted his hand to him and watched him go back into the house. He then looked up at the Moon. "The idea of going back is to the bed to sleep." He then drew himself from the chair and went into the house thinking that this time he'll be more- not so stressed from the ordeal as before. Going in the door of his bedroom, he thought, I was a living zombie. Maybe that was the idea.

Relaxed from a shower, Chris went to the bed and grabbed hold of his laptop. He adjusted the pillows behind him, and then leaned against the back on the bed. He researched body part transfers. And learned the meaning of a Procurement Company, this is where they sometimes go to and organs are kept alive on a ventilator. Then the different costs of body parts, he scrounged his face when he saw the sale of skin; it was used to enlarge penis size. Companies that store body parts are registered as non-profits, saying that they need this high amount of money just to keep the body parts alive.

Human organs have a 4-36 hour window to be kept alive; this is in the cold transfer. Preservation solutions help damage from happening by keeping the sodium and potassium levels in check. Temperatures from 32 to 39 degrees, the heart is most sensitive to blood flow. Kidneys are very resilient and can last 24 to 36 hours in cold storage, lungs last 6 to 8 hours, and the liver for about 12 hours.

Perfusion is hooking up a harvested organ to a machine that pumps oxygen and nutrient-rich fluid through the organ's tissues, as the heart would do in the body. While plugged into the machine, as the organ metabolizes energy and produces waste, its sugar stores are replenished, and toxic metabolites cleared away.

Before surgeons harvest an organ, the donor's heart stops pumping blood to the tissue for a period of time which causes the damage. Placing the organ in an organ in a perfusion machine may give the tissue a chance to recover. Cells use lactate during normal metabolic functions. lactate is a crude metabolic measure of perfusion through the body, but still serves superior compared to eyeballing a near-frozen organ for transportation. Still, some organs are still stored in ice/as high profusion costs.

India and the United Kingdom use warm profusion: lasts longer and less damage to organs, but it is not licensed in the U.S., yet. He scratches the top of his head. I have much more research to do. First of all, I have to find out, how old this information is I, I… (he stops his movement) feel like I am falling, but I am here. He bends over to the side of the bed and presses in his forehead. In one sudden awkward motion, he springs up off the bed and moving his arm to the side like he was swiping a sword at an enemy.

He lunges toward the door where this force seemed to come at him. Then he sharply turned his head and ran to the outside door of the bathroom and it opened wide. The only light was from the Moon and a few scattered stars. He ran to the center of the grass lawn. The two dogs woke up and started running and barking at him. This must-have had woken Bond because he was now there at the side of the grass watching Chris; he then leaned down and called the dogs. Only one came, he put it inside and closed the door.

These were moves that he was sure that his brother had done in some time of his life, but there was no one there other than the dog that now ran to Bond, he put this dog inside and closed the door as well. Chris seemed to be in an utter rage fighting for what Bond could see as only a non-existent being. He then thought with everything that has gone on, could this be a nightmare? More than anything he wanted to go to him and comfort him, but common sense told him that he had to stay away. Bond watched him more astutely to try and capture or reason to find out what and why he was doing this.

The outside light came on from the casita; Troy opened the door wide to find the reason for the noise. Bond waved his hand out to Troy then said, "Go back inside." Hearing this, Chris opened his eyes wide to Bond, like a tiger eyeing its prey. Fear engulfed Bond's body, he fought the needed desire to run inside and lock the door. Chris charged to Bond and was inches from touching him and hurling him to the ground. A bullet, the sound of a bullet pierced the air and Chris dropped. Bond looked to his brother stumbled on the grass, below his feet, then looked to the casita. Troy held a riffle in the air.

Bond wanted to yell at Troy, but this literally at that point saved his life. Bond then knew the answer to the question, P.T.S.D. He had just learned about it from what Jane was going through and now Chris. Bond bent down to hold him; he now looked like an animal who was begging for mercy from being taken to the lion's den. He gently placed his arms over him and for a moment just held them there. Chris raised his body up leaning to Bond. Troy was now there also helping, they got him back to bed.

Bond raised the sheets over his body on the bed and could see that he was trying to say something. He raised his finger to his mouth and made the sound of quiet, just go to sleep, everything will be alright. Chris closed his eyes, and then Bond sat on the easy chair in that room and closed his eyes to sleep.

# Chapter 25

A T 7:30 THE next morning Bond was sipping coffee, looking out the kitchen window, he saw something that he did not like. A minute later, Troy came in the kitchen saying, "Good morning" and heading for the refrigerator getting out a juice bottle. "I thought that you knew the rules here, and for that matter everywhere."

"Meaning what?"

"Meaning the female visitor that I saw leaving your casita."

"Oh, her, she is my regular." Bond choked while taking a sip, "You're regular, and you mean you do her or it, or never mind you know." Troy smirks replying he knows. Bond forcefully replied, "No more, not now, especially after what happened last night, speaking of that, was she here then?"

"No, not yet."

Sitting at the table, Troy peels a banana and hands one to Bond, he takes it. Bond holds it then moves it from side to side and sets it down. "I already had a hard-boiled egg; I just do not feel hungry." "What are our plans for today?" "Plans, plans, I haven't got any right now, with all of the changes that have happened and keep happening." The dog's bark and Bond ask him if he has fed them. No was the reply that he heard, "So, what are you waiting for, I am not going to do it." Troy leaves the table placing the half-finished banana and juice on the table and goes to the backyard.

"I don't want to, but I had better go check on Chris." In turning out of the kitchen to the hall, there stands Chris. "Why don't you want to?" he goes back to the kitchen then asks him if he knew what happened the night before, last night. "I did some work on information on my laptop, and then I guess I fell asleep. Why were there a pillow and a blanket on the chair in my room though?" Bond hands him a cup of coffee, Chris proceeds to put sugar in it then takes a sip. "You don't remember what you did last night? Being outside in the backyard, the dogs, me?"

Chris looked at him, especially after he said to me. "No, should I know something?" he leans back, "This is worse than I thought."

"Come on, with all that we have to do and all that I need to find out. Why would I be playing in the dark backyard at night? You need some more sleep." "Yes, I do need sleep, but even more now that you don't remember." Chris gave him a dirty look, then took a box of breakfast cereal from the cabinet and milk to the table, then took a bowl and proceeded to eat.

Bond went to the backyard; the dogs immediately ran to him barking with happiness. He played ball with them only for five throws, then paced back and forth by the swimming pool. "A swimming pool is sure a lot different from the ocean." his cell phone then beeped. Seeing that he had privacy he answered it. "Father, it is sure good to hear from you.

How are you doing?" he waited and listened to the answer, feeling happy that everything was fine, he then told his dad of the recent happenings with Chris. Hearing his father's response, he was very surprised. "So, take one to the airport and pick the other one up. Dad are you sure about this?" he hung up not even 10 seconds later. He raised his shoulders, and then showed a look of wonder, "If this is what he wants. So then, who am I going to be the? I hope not me."

Troy left for work. Bond drove the Mustang convertible with the top raised out of the garage, Chris was in the passenger seat. He said nothing to him, other than father wanted him back home in Hawaii. Especially since most everything was currently closed in Vegas: the gambling, the bars, the showgirls - everything more-or-less making Vegas. Chris didn't seem to put up any resistance to returning to the island estate. Bond then wondered about Chris's return, Jane will sure be happy about it, but the two of them both suffering from the same illness. Then he thought, with his return maybe that will cure her.

He stopped at the passenger drop off and started to get out to help him with his bags. Chris waved his hands no, then took everything and ran inside the airport. Bond was stricken at watching him leave, and in such a hurry. What were he thinking and why the quick escape? He checked his mirrors, then looked ahead again, then left the drove out of the airport to return back to "base" as he now called it. "There is something that I just don't know yet."

Almost home, he looked at the time on the console, "It'd already time for me to return there, I guess I should have parked and waited, but then that makes me a target." He took the next exit then circled around and got back on the freeway this time "to" the airport. This time he went to arrivals instead of dropping off. A familiar face waved to him then he stopped for this person to get in the car. "Jonathan, you look great!" Jonathan nodded fastening his seat belt. "Don't worry, this is going to be fun." Bond smiled at him then drove back to base, knowing the route pretty well by now.

Now inside the house, Jonathan viewed the dogs in the backyard and heard them bark. Bond placed a bottle of Pellegrino and glasses of ice on the table then asked him if he wanted to see the dogs. Jonathan replied, "No, I am allergic to dogs." Bond then stepped back and thought there was dog hair and dogs everywhere here. He said nothing, only sat to talk with Jonathan, about basically everything. The doorbell rang, Bond got up still reaching for his gun in apprehension, then not feeling one and thinking of where he was, but the fear sill did not escape him. It was fed ex. He answered and signed for it, then brought the large box in.

It does not have a name on it just this address though. It is from; it is from where you used to live, the condominium complex. Jonathan went to the box that Bond stood by. "Could your laptop with all the information that you said that you found out be there? I thought that it was still too dangerous to check on the place because probably too many police would be there, because of your absence, looking to see what happened to you." Jonathan said nothing in return; he just started opening the box. Bond watched him take things out. Some of his clothing, knickknacks, books, and then he stopped unpacking and stood up straight with a smiled on his face and returned to the kitchen table. Bond followed him wanting to know what this small box that he was holding.

Jonathan paused with the box laid on the table in front of him; he took a drink of water then smiled at Bond. This made Bond all the more nervous as to the outcome. You could tell that he had the nerves of a cat on a wire. Jonathan opened this box, and then held out a box of tea. "Tea, you mailed a box of tea, and this is making you almost elated."

"No, it is not the tea. It is what is in the tea box." He takes off the lid and tea bags fall to the tabletop. Bond looks even angrier. He then reaches inside the box and scrapes the side of it, and then pulls a USB. "A united serial bus." "What, a bus ticket?" "No, this is what it is," he opens his fingers and sees the USB, "all the information that you need that I have collected is here. I sensed that something like what did happen would. Oh, my laptop was on the kitchen table at the condominium, and it was taken. You see I took all of the information needed for this and left my laptop there with only games on it.

Something that would pass the time for shall I say older generation. Now, do you have a USB-C port?"

Bond did not know what the true meaning of what he asked him was; he just ran to his bedroom and took his laptop then went back to the kitchen. Jonathan plugged it in then pressed a few buttons. "Here, everything or all of the information that I have been able to retrieve so far is here." Bond started to reach for it, then thought better and got up and stood behind Jonathan to view it. "Your ring master's name is Horton T, Baxter." "Horton T, Baxter, I thought that he was locked up for life, in San Quentin."

"Apparently, he escaped. I don't know how, but he has been out for over a month now." "And he came to Vegas?" "Oh, he has a major operation going to get more money than ever thought possible, nothing compared to gambling, or prostitution, or drugs. But I suppose in a way you could say it is related to drugs." "Related, how so?" "Medical." "Medical, what bandages?" "Your brother was on to this." "Chris knew something and he didn't tell me about it that just does not sound right and it's not right." "Have you checked his room?" "No, I left there this morning, but." "You left there this morning, why were you there this morning, with him?" "The episode that he had last night, I stayed there and slept on the chair in that room that he was in to make sure that he wouldn't do anything again. I woke up long before him."

Jonathan said nothing, he just looked at him. Seeing no response, he replied, "Go check," and he followed. They're right in the middle of the room and saw the unmade bed, the ruffled blanket on the easy chair. A glass of water on the nightstand and on the floor to the side of the bed, a laptop, and a note pad with Chris's writing in it on what he had found out. Bond picked up the notepad and saw various information that Chris had written on organ transfer. He read it over, Jonathan picked up the laptop. "He was busy last night I guess before his whole incident happened."

They each go back to the dining room table. Looking puzzled Bond takes a sip of water, and then looks to Jonathan." Most of all that the research that your brother did was on the present-day way America work as far as organ transfer, cold organ transfer. But today's or the world's technology has led us to our society to "Warm Organ Transfer," "looking over his notes, as they now do it in Iran, Australia, and the United Kingdom. So, this is where he is getting the money, back-market organ transfers?" Jonathan shakes his head. "You can see what happened to me. He does have connections, this is very risky, well most all situations that 'You' encounter are risky, but this one is everybody, involved or not. Some lives greatly matter, others do not. And ours my friend do not."

Bond then looks like he is right in the game ready to play. "Jonathan, do you think that my dad knows?" Jonathan tilts back, takes a drink of water followed by another one. "Why do you think that you are here?" Bond then shows a look of further importance. "We're in the middle of this now, aren't we?" "Yes, you are." Bond immediately picked up on the meaning of that.

# Chapter 26

INSIDE THE 14TH floor penthouse, Unit D is Horton T. Baxter, laid out on a chaise lounge holding a Jack Daniels on ice, looking out of the lights of the city. More graying hairs have grown on his beard and mustache contrasting his jet-black hair that is thinning, giving him a higher forehead mark for hair to start growing. Somehow the tarnish of the sunlit city escaped him, showing his still pale skin. Creepy skin had invaded his arms. And the large bones of his frame showed through to his thin frame. Shiny thick gold rings adorned every finger, but his thumbs making a punch by him is more painful.

Slow rap music, if there could be such a thing filled the airwaves of the room. His assistant called him to the table for a steak dinner with baked potatoes; he declined to say that he wanted only to think about his plans and how to carry them out. The rap music stopped, and then he felt uneasy in the cold solitude of the silent room. He did get up and go to the dining table. He took a serrated steak knife and held it up before him. He softly felt the sharp edges of the blade of the knife and smiled. "You could use this for more than just one thing." He then grinned from ear to ear. his assistant that was already well into eating this dinner, then commented that it was sure a lot different than the meals served in San Quentin. He held the knife tight in his hand clamping it closed and squeezing the very tightest that he could until his fingers turned red. He widened his eyes and looked directly into his man's view, "YOU!

We are never to talk about that again!!! You got me, or there Will be consequences!"

Then his assistant looked up to him, then back down to the plate in front of him and non- clemently replied, "Okay," then continued eating his meal. "Presently we are doing well, but there is always better to do and that I will." He stopped to chewing a large bite of the filet Mignon. "There is a great need and a greater supply that I can always get too." rap music again started playing. He looked more than delighted and ate all that he could enjoy every bite, chewing hard. He took one small break from chewing and eating. "It is going to be a nice night." He then overshadowed the sound of the music with unique sinister laughter.

# Chapter 27

TROY DROVE TO the gates of the storage facility and was surprised when his card and code did not open the gate. He was checking in 20 minutes before opening so there shouldn't have been any customers trying to get in yet. The glare of the morning sun was especially strong that morning, even when he squints his eyes and cover the top of them with his finger, he still could not make out a view of the office. He had a key ring, so he unlocked the gate himself, and then punched the code. The only thing that could go wrong was the burglar alarm going off. He hoped in his mind that unlocking the main lock and punching in the code did this otherwise there was going to be a large problem.

The gate opened now closer only twelve feet from the office, he could see that Larry's truck was there. What was the problem? He was very concerned, the number one thing that he feared was if Larry would be alive being this solemn mood lately. Before getting out of the jeep he waved his hand over his face reminding himself of identity change and of how he was going to have to maintain it for the rest of the day. He got out and then checked his footing before walking to the office with his thermos and plastic lunch pail in hand.

Inside the office, he could hear only the squeaky door hinge close behind him. No one sat behind the counter, he then thought trying to calm his heartbeat, and maybe he is just in the bathroom. Sure enough, 30 seconds later he came out of the bathroom door. He did look surprised at seeing him; Troy thought this odd because he had never seen Larry act this way in his presence before. In the dopiest vice that he could speak, he asked Larry if he was okay. Larry replied yes, just a headache, and he didn't sleep that well, it was nothing; he didn't want to hear about it all today. Troy just bent down conveying that he understood.

Troy went to the back at the side of the counter and put away his things. He did open his lunch box, then close it and handed Larry an orange. "I bought a bag of them at the store-had one last night, it sure was good, brought one for you, too." Larry took it from his hand and lowered his head silently, his eyes started to well with tears though none were shed. "No one has ever…" he turned his body away from his view. "Hurry up and get to work. I am not paying you to stand around." Troy said nothing, he just went out the door and to the Cushman to start his morning drives around the grounds.

During the day helping people open their units, sweeping and checking on things, etc., he thought of Larry and the desperate state that he was in that morning and then he thought that he was reading too much into it. Maybe someone in the family died or something like that. He was never what you'd call a life of the party anyway. It is just a matter of how to get to and see what the dealings were in that one building. He thought mostly today of all days to stay away from it because the trucks had been going to that unit all day and many times during it. They never seemed to stay for more than 15 minutes tops.

There was just something about that day; things had gone on as usual, except for Larry's mood and the constant coming and going of these large trucks. He then thought all the more reason to ignore it and go on with the day. Bond warned him that they might try and set up some kind of trap if they suspected anything. At the end of the workday, Troy asked Larry if he needed help closing up. Larry looked lost in thought and trapped in his mind. Troy had to repeat asking him the question. He still looked puzzled.

"It's that time already?" "Where do I go?" "Ah, does that mine, I have to drop you off to go grocery shopping or something?" "Ha, what…yeah, I have to be somewhere. The truck has been acting up any way. Just give me a ride." Troy nodded his head and they left, stopping at the gate to lock up,

Troy did it for him. He left him off at a small grocery store in a complex. Larry got out and even forgot to close the door behind him when he left. Troy watched him leave as he walked away with no direction just to the front of the store and stood there. He bent forward toward the door, was able to grab the handle and pulled it closed. Driving away home, he thought another mystery. He laughed to himself and said aloud dinner conversation.

Now back at home base. Troy parks at the end of the drive and goes to the side gate. He is instantly met by wagging tails. "Yes, I am happy to see you two too." He goes inside the casita, changes clothes. Now just a pair of shorts and a loose tee-shirt, he throws the ball for the dogs then fills their food bowls and water then goes inside the main house.

He sees Bond making a salad for dinner. "What do we have here?" he looks to Bond and the counter while saying this. "A Cobb salad," "That's old." "Yeah, you don't see it on many menus anymore."

Bond turns to the counter behind him and asks Troy to bring it to the table. Bond goes to it with a pitcher of ice water, and then sits down. They both help themselves to the food and water. Troy stops eating and asks Bond, "What did you do today?" "A little surfing," Troy looks at him questioning the answer, "Surfing on the web. Our man in charge of this operation, the one who rents out the entire storage building B is." He starts chewing again. At just that moment Jonathan enters the room holding a plate then sits down and serves himself some. He proceeds to take the conversation. "Phoenix enterprises rents it. The man in charge of the head of Phoenix enterprise is Horton T, Baxter." Troy drops his fork on his plate. "He was put away years ago for that horrific crime and is in prison." Bond interjects, "Apparently not. Oh, and Jonathan this is Troy, Troy, Jonathan." They both look at each other and nod their heads. Jonathan then sits down and helps himself to the food.

"Did you find anything else out?" he looks to Bond for the answer. Jonathan interjects, "Don't you think it's a bit odd that he escaped and no media attention to it? He is here in Vegas, and took over a bankrupt company and no one is questioning any of it?" We are saying, Troy. "Exactly! That is why he cannot know anything about us." "They have already found. They are suspicious of something." "Why haven't the police found them?" Bond pushes back his chair a bit, then rubs his hands down his thighs takes a breath in then replied, "Connections and this is maybe not what we have to find out but something that we have to work around."

"The two spots we have are that hospital and the storage facility and for some reason, Chris put it in his notes that bar, lucky. We need to find out where Horton lives and where is he working from." Jonathan in his elegant voice speaks out, "Wouldn't the headquarters of this business the enterprises, be the same if they just took it over." "No, it is not, which seems strange in itself. Now, instead of being on the north side of town, it is on the east side." He leans back then smiles, "I think that I have a connection and that she can help me, here with this." The two other men smile to him then proceed with dinner.

# Chapter 28

CHRIS LEAVES THE limo at the front of the estate in Hawaii. He tips the driver then watches it leave out the gate. He drops his bag to the ground, and then walks to the right side of the outside of the property instead of heading into the house. It looks like he is taking surveillance- he then goes to the front door of the house. In that moment he appears lost. He lifts his hand to the knob, at first barely touching it then takes hold of it in a tight motion instantly turns looking behind him then opens it wide. NO one is here; he shows reluctance to being there. He quietly goes inside and places his bags to the side near the base of the stairs. He stands there looking at nothing. Then goes into the living room and pours himself a drink. He sits on the couch but instead of looking at the view out the window, he looks at the floor. He mumbles words of no distinction-speaking only to himself. He looks up to see his empty glass and goes and pours himself another going back to sit right where he was before. Did he think maybe I should look for dad, but then why? He sent for me, he should find me.

He says to himself; no one wants me, I have to hide. I just am not here. He goes to his bag, but instead of going upstairs to the bedroom that he did share with Jane, he goes to Bond's bedroom on the main floor in the back, away from everything. Before leaving for this room, he side-circles and goes back into the living room and takes the entire bottle of liquor.

The only thing that follows him is sheer quietness and solitude.

Opening the door to the room, he did not go inside instead he throws the bag in the room and it lands on the right side of the bed. After taking a full view of the room and then looking at his bag, he steps inside and then closes the door rapidly then holds his hand firmly on the knob looking at the knob like he was going to move. He jumps back and stares at the door. Stepping around his suitcase he stops at the door to the bathroom. It is ajar, he hides behind it, then looks inside as if he was looking for enemies, not seeing anyone there, he breathes out and takes his jacket off, throwing it to the floor. Sweeping the top of the bed, and then looking under the bed linens on it seeing nothing under the bed, he sighs then somewhat smiles. He takes off all but his underclothes then get under the sheets, pulling them tightly just under his chin. He can feel his heart race in panic and desperately tried to sleep where in 10 minutes he was in a locked state of sleep, to him this is now sheltered.

Jane walks down the stairs and sniffs the air. She walks in a spinning path leading her nowhere but still is captivated by this scent. Vincent then comes into the room and smiles at seeing her. He notices her locked state of confusion and asks her if she is alright. She replies yes, but still is noticeably captivated by something; she looks as if something is just not right. He sits down, looks at the time on his wristwatch, then to the front door. He sees that she still appears to be in a state of grief. He calls her over, she declines and then walks to the outside door and looks out. "It is just not the same, I mean I can't go out and wait for him anymore." In her action, she runs back up the stairs crying.

Vincent sits back on the couch looking to the movement of the ocean, and then softly says to himself, "And now there are going to be two. Bond, I need you. I cannot wait until Maggie comes back from her vacation." He breathes out hard and then takes his hand to his chest. He tries getting up, then falls back down to the couch. He breaths in attempting this again and still falls back down, he looks out to the crashing waves. "What am I... No.?" he reaches to the top of the coffee table places and hand on it, then bends forward with his other hand bracing the couch and finds momentum to stand. He then stands looking out not noticing the view, braced against nothing he turns, and heads back to his bedroom, saying in his mind, he had better go take a pill and rest on his bed. When Chris comes home, he'll let me know.

The three of them were all home at this one place to be together, but mentally were miles apart.

Chris had awakened from a dream. A dream he did not like, he was running from someone and he couldn't remember what he was running to or what he was looking for. He rose out of bed, then fell to sitting on the bed, with both hands he grabbed his forehead, he trembled, shaking, crying, mumbling, then screamed, "Why, why?" he turned white and tensed up then ran to the bathroom and threw up in the toilet. Each time that he rose up his head he hurled it back down to throw up. After what seemed minutes of this he reached to the wall and raised his body. Then turned the shower on and waited for the water to warm, he looked in the mirror expressing a look of "who am I". Awakened back to reality hearing the pounding jets of the shower, he disrobed and got in standing, unmoved and crying.

Inside her bedroom, Jane took her hands to each side of her head, feeling her hair and slowly ever so slowly released them. "What do I do now? I was brought here to reunite with him, then once he is here and we are happy he is sent away; now I even think that I can even smell him. When I do, I am alone in every sense of the word. Not even Lauren is here. Well, that may be good for her as she is off living at the dorm in college. I hope she is happy and Bond, Bond… I could talk to him about anything and he knew, he knew, he was my lifeline, my security and now he is gone. I am so alone."

She walks over to the stereo, then foils through the albums. She stops on Meatloaf, and then pulls the record out of the case. Turns on the machine and places the needle down, waiting to hear it. It plays. "Oh, that is only fitting, 'Two out of three isn't bad, and right I know'," she stops and breathes out, "and right now, ever so appropriate. In only seconds she is belting her heart out to the music.

Chris now out of the shower and dressed ever so nicely: a short-sleeve Hawaiian print button shirt, loose black shorts and sandals. Looking in the mirror and then smiling, he leaves the room then walks into the living room and sees that it is empty. He goes to the kitchen and takes a bottle of beer from the refrigerator, then goes to the outside patio expressing happiness.

Vincent slowly walks to the kitchen to pour himself a glass of ice water, then stops scratching his arm and sighs. In even slower steps he heads to the outside patio. Upon sitting at the table, he sees an open bottle of beer and wonders why. Then from the beach Chris walks forward to him. He opens and closes his eye, wondering if he truly sees him or if he is dreaming. Feeling a strong hand on his shoulder, he knows that it is not a dream and Chris is there. He lifts his lowered body state and sits back straightening up on the chair and smiles to him. "It is sure good to see you, father, I have been worried about you." "I AM glad that you are here, I have been worried about you as well." Chris stands telling a look of surprise and ask why, raising his hands open in the air.

"Well, it is the fourth of July and, ah…let me just say I didn't want to be alone." "Isn't my wife here?" Vincent thinks strongly about the answer to his question feeling with a sense of the matter she isn't. "Ah, yes she is, I just haven't seen that much of her lately." "Speaking of that, where is she?" "I am sure that she is upstairs, maybe getting ready to see you, don't be surprised if she runs off when she does see you." "Why would she run from me?" Vincent takes a sip of water, and then collapses with hands, "Just happiness."

# Chapter 29

T HE FOLLOWING MORNING in Vegas, Bond is already outside holding a cup of coffee, walking around the swimming pool. He hears a click and takes his cell phone out from his pant pocket, sets the coffee down on a chair and reads it. "We're on, I had better get there quick." He leaves for the city planning department. Of course, being the 4th of July, the office is closed, but on the side parking lot he can still see a few scrambled cars in the parking lot. He answers a text message on his phone, and then steps to the side of the building. At first it looks to be a garden with a high five-foot green leafy plant, a side door is opened, he runs in. He smiles to Laurie. She is dressed professionally and is displaying her name badge. "Hurry, we only have 20 minutes until the cameras start a new cycle as they are now changing the batteries and re-testing them." She walks down a hall, then unlocks two portioned glass doors with wooded frame and leads him in locking it back up after they're inside. At a half wooden swinging door, she stops then unlocks and goes inside. Bond waits at the customer counter.

"I made paper copies of all of the records of the sale of Phoenix enterprises and the businesses that pertain to it." "I'll walk you out, but leave and leave now, I cannot lose this job." She quickly walks him out and doesn't even look up to see him leave as she re- locks the side door. Once at the end of the plants of the small cement walkway. He takes three steps forward, then turns in circles and walks further to the right opposite the way that he entered. He looks up to the sun, then squints looking back down to the cement ground that he stands on. A security guard riding an electric standing bike, then stops at his side and asks him why he is there, the building is closed. He replies that he was just looking for a Starbuck's, in seeing the large building there he thought one would be there. The officer then tells him no and points to the west direction telling him down four blocks and to his right on the corner there would be one. He thanked him, then walks away, first stopping at a park bench making it look like he was tying his shoe making sure that the officer was out of view before going back to his car.

"Now back to base, hopefully Jonathan and I can find something out. And Troy is back at the storage facility, so much there needs to be explored. Well, two good leads, that is good news, but first, where is this Starbuck's?" he drives put of the parking lot and follows the verbal directions that the officer gave him. Parked at the lot of Starbuck's he gets out of his car, then goes to the door, and more than surprised and happy that there were only two people in line. He ordered a non-fat latte and paid for it, then stopped at the door before opening it and took a sip. He licks the foam off of his upper lip and replied, "Oh I needed that." Driving out of the parking Bond wonders how it is going with Troy at the storage facility. He then thinks that he wants ever so much just to have a minute or so, he reaches over and turns the radio to a soft rock station, the Beatles," let It Be", plays.

He remarks aloud, that has to be one of the very best songs ever written. He walks inside "base" singing out the lyrics. "Whisper words of wisdom, let it be." He stops on seeing Jonathan with solemn face sitting watching the news on the television. "What is wrong?" Jonathan breaths in then let out the air, the second he has done doing this he says, "100 people have died here in Nevada today from COVD19." Bond's expression and feeling is then instantly wiped from his body. Jonathan sees the look of despair from Bond. He turns off the television and goes to the kitchen table. He puts on his eyeglasses then asks Bond what he has found out. Bond opens the papers he had just got and hands them to Jonathan. Jonathan reads it over then sets it down.

Bond looks at him waiting for any news from him. "The funny thing is… (he stops) the purchase was made before the company filed for bankruptcy." "How can that be, the reason that they sold was that they did go bankrupt." "Maybe they knew that they were and they already made plans on who to sell to." Bond leans back looking very disturbed, "You mean that something was already planned, and it works? This was supposed to have happened. Somebody knew something." "Somebody or some people, and also, your (he stops and takes off his eyeglasses) Mr. Horton has acquired 15% of the hospital-to date." "How, you don't make that kind of money in prison." "Maybe, maybe not, he seems to have pulled," "With who?" "After looking at this, a lot of different places and the right places." Bond sighs, put his arms on the chair and put forward, a look of utter defeat.

Both Jonathan and his cell phone beep with a message from Troy. They look at each other then Bond reads the message. He says aloud to Jonathan, "It just says to call him." Jonathan tells him to make the call. "Yes, hi Troy, what is it?" he pauses to hear Troy's response, "he is dead?" Jonathan looks over and reaches for the phone. Bond holds it closer to his ear. "Yes, yes, we'll be right there, for now just keep the body out of view and do not say anything to anyone." They each get up and leave looking intently to the other." "Plan B, yes plan B."

Troy anxiously waits for their arrival. He was constantly checking the monitor of the security gate and looking out the window, even opening the door and looking out. He looks to his wristwatch, then goes back behind the counter and checks the time on the wall clock. "No difference." He walks down the side hall and stops in the men's room where he put Larry's body. He sees a couple walk into the office, they are talking away to each other so he cannot guess as to what they want. All of a sudden, the man stops and the woman looks at him with interest. He reaches in his pocket. Troy's heart jumps. He is reaching for a gun. He runs behind the counter and ducks down. The sound of the door swinging open, he grasps for and swallows hard, bent on his knees behind the counter. Then this woman's voice is heard, "Is anybody here?" She gets no response, so she asks again in a louder voice. The man then replies, "I'm going to use the bathroom." Troy jumps up and goes to the side of the hallway shielding this man from making a move toward it, "Sorry, but the bathroom is out of order." He places each hand on the edge of the wall of the hall. The man gruffly sighs. The woman then says that they are simply bringing a check for that month's payment and she hoped that there would not be a late fee. He tells them to thank you, and it would be okay, he'd take care of it. He opens his arm to the door and walks there more or less pushing them out all the while telling them to have a nice day.

He instantly checks his wristwatch again, "Now I have to use the restroom. When are they going to get here?" he places a sign on the door "back soon", then locks it, and uses the woman's room. Coming out he is wiping his hands on a paper towel. Then lifts his hand to his nose, "Their soap smells better." The phone rings, he then explains the cost of the rent there to the person on the phone. Right before he can say goodbye, the phone from the gate bell rings. He walks nervously around the room holding the phone waiting for the smallest invitation to end the call. Finally, he just breaks in and says goodbye, then looks at the monitor and sees that it is a large moving van, a different one than what the Phoenix enterprises uses. Answering the phone, he hears a familiar voice then presses the button to release the gate. The van drive in then drives past the office, turns and now has the back of the large truck open right at the door of the office.

Two large Mexican men get out, and then open the roll up in the back of the truck all the way. He unloads a couch, and then walks to Troy bringing it in the office. They unwrap it from the entire heavy plastic wrap encasing it, then rolls the plastic wrap back up and close the roller door of the back and lock it. One goes back to Troy who now stands outside. He signs a clipboard and it leaves. Troy noticed that a few of the people there watched this happen. He looks to his wristwatch again, and then goes back to the office. After he is inside a moment later, he looks out to see if anyone is driving in the gate. Seeing nothing, he huffs then goes back to the office.

The van that made the delivery gets on the freeway and heads south, and then takes the second exit, rolling right in the back of a large truck fuel stop. They look at each other than the driver checks his wristwatch in the parking spaces on each side of them are clear. The passenger sees a truck pull to the side then one park on the driver's side as well. The engines of each truck stop, both the driver and passenger look at the other. Then the passenger pulls up a leather bag, unzips and sees wades of cash, hundred-dollar bills.

A man is wearing a baseball hat over his face to hide his eyes, dressed in medium blue pants and shirt goes to the side of the passenger. And he is handed the leather bag. They both nod their head. He is then handed a key to the lock-in back and unlocks it taking out the large plastic roll that they left the storage unit with. The key is then handed back to him and each truck leaves. The center moving truck then gets back on the freeway and heads north.

The passenger asks the driver if they can make the very first safe stop that they can. He nods his head to him. They end up going back to the truck yard where they rented this truck from. The driver goes inside and hands back the keys, a man comes out and checks the truck and the mileage. When all is good, he goes back inside his office and they get in a regular street van. Inside of it they go in the back and change their clothes and pull off the face masks and pull off their gloves. Bond then sits behind the wheel and Jonathan rides shotgun. He turns to Bond and asks, "Can we go home now?" Bond snickers then say "yes".

"Where are they going to take the body? Ah, Larry" "Well, it turns out that he didn't really have a sister here in the city, in fact nowhere. He was long divorced and he just got the news that his former wife died, this was one of the reasons why he was so quiet and forlorn and no other living family." "What about his burial?" "He, Larry, will get a full proper burial in Utah, St. George." "But that will be reported, so anyone can find this out here, and you know who, I mean." "Ahead of you on that, it seems for some reason he never went by his real name. Everyone just called him Larry, he was paid by cash for his work, and he paid his landlord cash. He had no credit cards." "You can't survive in this world today with them even an ATM card. Is it possible?" Bond tilted his head and makes a questionable expression, "As hard to believe, some folks actually have, and he was one of them." "What was his real name?" "Alexander Bell." "He must have been razed by that; I can see why he changed his name."

# Chapter 30

J ANE CAME DOWN the stairs and not sensing Vincent inside, she went outside. Chris instantly smiled at her and ran to her and hugged her. She started crying, "Are you really here?" "Yes, babe I am," "Babe? Who are you calling babe? I am not babe. Who have you been seeing, I am your wife, not babe!" he stands back from her, "Gee, I am sorry I just meant it as a good thing." She looks down at Vincent. He has no idea what to say to her and is surprised by her demeanor. She turns to walk back in the house, then abruptly stops, then goes to walk the shoreline. He looks at Vincent. He waves his arms signaling that he doesn't know. Chris goes to the shoreline to follow her. Vincent can't understand why she didn't just embrace him and not let him go. "This is going to take time for this to play out and tonight should have been so very good." Chris made to where she was walking, he followed her footprints and then stopped right behind her as she had stopped in motion, and she turns around then looks to him eye to eye. "You are not Bond." "No, I am your husband, Chris, remember?" "What, no you are just in my mind, you are not here, or are you?" he very carefully opens his hands to her, "I am here, I am your husband, I am Chris." He stands there silently and waits for her to do or say anything. She looks at him like she has been betrayed, then closes her eyes and lowers her head. Then in very slow motion, she pulls herself up to look at him, looking at his face, she sees it is him. She drops her body in his arms and cries out, "You are here, and you are really here. Thank the good lord, you are here." And then holds him ever so tightly. He embraces her in return.

Vincent sees this and then smiles, "It is about time." They then walk back up to the patio, smile to Vincent then go upstairs forgetting dinner, at least for the moment. Vincent watches this, and then huffs in response, "I guess that I am eating alone tonight." He rises up from the chair and enters the house. "This is a very good thing though, I am glad. I hope that they watch the fireworks later or (he laughs) maybe they are making their own".

# Chapter 31

THEY STOP AT In-out drive-thru getting much-needed food. Jonathan finishes taking a sip of soda, then asks Bond what the next step in the plan was, though he already had an idea of what it was.

Bond finishes his last bite of a cheese-burger and reaches over to pull one more handful of animal fries, "Plan B." "Do you have what I need?" "Troy does." Next thing, they pull into the storage facility. Parking at the side of the office, Bond can already see Troy nervously looks out the window for them, he checks the rear-view mirror then gets out of the van Jonathan does well. He pulls the side door open then takes a large cardboard box in the office.

"Where were you two? It has been such a long time." Bond sets the box down. "Oh, we had a nice round of golf." "You're kidding, right?" Bond just smiled then says looking down to the box, "A little help here." Jonathan opens the swinging half-door, and then Troy helps him bring the box around to the back. "Guess what, you are coming home." "Jonathan, I know, there is a small bedroom on the back and everything that I need is right there." They say goodbye but before they leave Troy locks the gate.

Now inside the house, Troy as usual plays with the dogs in the backyard then feeds them. Bond looks out the back-kitchen window to see this. He stretches then goes to his bedroom. Standing behind the closed door, he huffs as he sees that he can't sit on the edge of the bed as he was accustomed to. He takes off his tee shirt now wearing a tank undershirt and he slides to the floor holding his cell phone then dials his number in Hawaii.

He nervously taps his knee as he hears the ring tone. His father answers the call in a sleepy voice.

"Dad, are you alright?" his father says fine that was just turning in for bed. "I know of the time difference, but it is still a bit early, isn't it?" "Yes, the two of them, are…well in their bedroom." "Are they okay, I mean is Chris okay?" "He wasn't at first, but last that I did see him, he was very composed as he usually is." Bond breathed out a sigh of relief hearing that. "Well, thanks dad, you take care, I love you."

"Love you too, good night." As his father spoke these last words to him, he could hear his voice lighten and slow. He hoped that this was only because of sleep.

"A shower sure sounds good right now." He circled his room, and then remembered no bathroom adjacent in his room. Hum, he walks down the hallway to the bathroom and showers. At the very first feeling of the cascading drops hitting his skin, he sighed out, welcoming the feeling of relief that this momentarily gave him. Now wrapped in a towel going back in his room, he said aloud, "Better than a beer."

Now walking down the limited hallway area, he hears the doorbell ring. He instantly frowned and took a guard stance. He hears the door open and called out to Troy. Hearing the response of "Yeah" eased his apprehension. Troy was holding a bag. "I sent out for Chinese food." Bond instantly went to the kitchen to get plates and forks. Troy told him that the beers were already on the table. Bond opened a container with a happy expression, Troy saw this and felt happy.

"Let's see what do we have here? Moo Shoo Pork, vegetable lo Mein, crab rangoon's and chicken fried rice, good choices." Troy responds the usual. "We've completed step one." Bond nods his head, "Yes and it went easier than I thought which worries me, it will be just tomorrow." "Tomorrow, what is tomorrow?" "This remains to be seen." "And tonight, being the fourth, are we going to go out and view the fireworks? They always have a beautiful display on the strip." "Oh, (he sighs) I forgot about that." He scratches his head and leans back. Troy reaches for more rice. "I don't want to walk into a landmine, sorry but we're staying here." He was surprised to see no upset response from Troy then asks him why. He tells him there is always next year.

That evening was spent sitting on the chairs in the backyard with the dogs viewing them in the shy. At a little after ten, they went back in because of the extreme amount of smoke in the skies making it hard to breathe. Standing at the door of the casita Troy says to Bond, "Are we calling it a night then," Bond shakes his head and then says good night at the door; the dogs whine at the doors and whimper hearing the sound of the fireworks. He looks down at them with their ears down and begging eyes, "I suppose that you want to come in?" They each ran in the side of the open door that whisked Bond back, "Good thing that I was holding on to it."

They ran to the door of the empty master bedroom; he saw this and opened the door, and then told them that he is not in there. Before he knew it, they were both lying on the bed, one on each side. "Where does your master ever sleep? I guess I lodged in between you two some way. Good night you two." He then closes the door and goes to his room. He climbs the bed, and then looks for comfort hearing the ever increasing noise and banging of the fireworks. Each individual pop makes him want to grab his gun in retaliation, each forthcoming bang makes him quiver and feel dangling nerves run down his spine. Fear grips his mind in every respect. In a desperate motion, he gets out of bed and wraps himself in the comfort of the bed sheets then heads to the hallway. The dogs each whimper at his side. "Sorry guys, this is bothering me too." He turns on the television, seeing mostly only info-commercials. "Probably because of the time, they still expect everyone to still be outside; I would be if it weren't for this horrific noise." A knock on the back door is then heard, the dogs instantly bark, he knows that any noise from the ordinary would have already wakened up Troy. In opening the door, he found it was Troy, who was surprisingly calm.

"Doesn't all this extremely loud noise affect you? It is sure bothering me and the dogs." "It did for a while, and then I did something about it." "Want to have another beer?" "Something better than CBD oil." He bends to each of the dogs and rubs some in the side of their gums, then gives some to Bond. "I do the same thing, more-or-less. How do you know about this, never mind?" Bond then uses some. He sees the skeptical look on his face, then says just give it a while. "The noises are still so loud, does this happen every year here?" "No, I guess that this year is a lot worse, the worse than it has ever been because of people being and feeling so sheltered because of the lockdown for the virus." "That makes sense."

"Look at your news there, the killings and the shootings, the protesting." Bond then sits down to watch it, "My God, they are even firing at children, and they can't know what they're doing." "And burning the American flag?" "God, if they don't like it here, go to another country and see what it is like there." "They are only making this whole thing worse, and worse for the American tax-payer which is them. No police? Who are they going to call when someone points a gun at their home or their family? Or a burglary or a rape" "I don't know, right now it just looks like utter destruction and anarchy." "How are we going to fix this?" "By just being us, and not changing to the present view of them," "You are right, peaceful." loud puncturing sonic bangs fill the air. Bond bends forth off of the chair and bends over sheltering himself. "This is too much, it is midnight. When is this going to end?" he then gets himself up and looks to the television. It showed a loud pop and then a large building blew-up. "Is this here?" "I don't know, let's try and listen." The commentator of the news voice is then heard. "A huge warehouse on the east side of Vegas was just blown up. It is too early for the police to do any kind of investigation because of the intense burning. If you are in this area, stay away." "Is that?" "No, Jonathan is okay; he is on the west side remembered. But that, (he goes to the kitchen table and looks at some papers, then holds them up) that warehouse our friend Horton owns. He is covering his tracks, evidently there is or was something there that he didn't want anyone to find out what it was." Chris then remarks, "Or somebody." "Oh God, we are in for it, and right in the middle." "Right now, the entire world is in chaos." Just as he finished this sentence another piercing loud firework exploded in the air. Yet, they each had become numb to the sound.

"Maybe, we should try and turn in?" The sound of the dogs snoring then is heard and they gently laugh. "After hearing and feeling all of the news, I feel like staying here, but I should still be in my place in case there is any unwanted company during the night." They each tip their head to the other. Bond lay like a corpse on the bed with open eyes. "There are still sounds of fireworks, I just feel much calmer now, and I hope that sleep will settle in soon." Before he could even think of what he was going to say to himself next he was in a state of restful sleep.

# Chapter 32

THE MORNING WIND made it impossible to be outside in this otherwise sunny morning in Hawaii. Vincent answered the door to Maggie; they each smiled at the other and were very happy to again be working together. He asked her about her vacation and she explained it all to him while having coffee in the kitchen. Chris came without saying anything, he looked to them both then poured two cups of coffee and returned upstairs. After he was out of the room, Maggie said, "Talkative, isn't he?" Vincent didn't want to elaborate on it and stayed quiet.

Vincent did some therapy with Maggie then went to his office to check on the situation in Las Vegas on his computer. He sat back quietly rubbing his hands together searching for an answer that he didn't have. "More than anything right now I wish that I was thirty years younger and I could be there." He reached up and ran his open hand over his face then sighed. The sad thing is that Chris doesn't even realize what is happening to him. "Denial is one of the steps of grief, what his wife is going through and right now with PTSD I just have to keep him away from basically everything and everyone. He has already had these outbursts and he probably doesn't even remember. Bond, I need you right now, he does too."

To get his mind off of this he looks back to his computer. "How to crush a Phoenix, they rise up from the ashes even more powerful than before?" he looks solemn and lost lowering his head. Then rise up looking at first to the ceiling, then straight ahead. "Become a more powerful Phoenix." He gets up, then leaves his office going to the living room looking out to the ocean. "My son, Bond you can do it." Chris stands at the base of the stairs, sees and hears this.

Chris goes back up the stairs, feeling hopeless about him and just lowers his body to sit on the floor right next to the door of his bedroom. "I do not want to be found, if anyone is looking for me. I am lost." He then shed a visible tear looking numb to the world.

# Chapter 33

JONATHAN LEAVES THE back bedroom of the office. Then turns the computer on, turns on the lights, disconnects the alarm, turns on the phones, then unlocks the office door to outside. He sips his morning coffee while turning on the wall TV. He looked happy until hearing the morning news. Viewing it for 10 more minutes he eventually turned it off and opted for the sound of the track music instead.

Two guests then enter the office; the sound of a bell is heard as they walk through the open door. Jonathan does not look up; he waits until he sees a hand on the counter to raise his head. He looks at them waiting for a response without smiling, as Larry would have done. Horton with his guard standing to the side of him are there looking very surprised at seeing Larry. "You are here!" he looks at them solemnly, "Where else would I be?" Horton looks perplexed, and then pushes over a wad of bills to him on the counter. He raises one eyebrow, and then moves his lips to the side saying something. They leave once out the door, he looks back in the office then they depart in their SUV.

Jonathan watches them leave through the monitor, once he sees the gate close, he takes a plastic bag and reaches for the wad of cash placing it in the bag then lifts and seals it. Troy comes expressing happiness seeing Larry then realizes that it is indeed Jonathan dressed and portraying Larry, all part of the plan.

He waits to be handed the keys to the Cushman then leaves the office. Riding around the lot he thinks to himself just another day, keep it simple. Probably the least said the better. The day progressed in the normal fashion.

Bond dressed in the doctor scrubs one more time, and went back to the hospital using his limited medical knowledge when necessary, and paying special attention to everything. The one thing that greatly consumed was when an operation was going on full well then suddenly, the patient's vials dropped without apparent reason. Instead of being called and the time of death recorded he was wheeled out of the O.r. while still having all necessary tubes, oxygen and blood to keep him alive. The staff wheeled his gurney was then reduced down to one. He unlocked a side wall door then it instantly locked behind him.

Bond then thought, the hospital has to know about this or maybe not, only a small working few knew, but then why hasn't this been discovered by anyone? The pandemic and the velocity in which they all have to work but still. Where are they taking this patient body and what is going to be done with it? He quickly walks back to view the name on the O.r. screen. An orderly is already there. He looks at him. The first thing that he does think of is he has nothing to bribe him with, then quickly asks him what the name was on the patient that just left the O.r. "I don't know." "Come on, you just took the name off; they can't be cleaning the room yet." The orderly then says, "I just want to get on with my day; his name was John Smith, no middle initial. Okay?" he then takes what is in his hand and leaves down the hallway behind him. Bond then thinks, that name, was it real or a cover-up being such a simple name to be maybe a diversion that did have meaning to them, whoever, the "Them" are.

He then thought of "Laurie" but different records. What is the system that the hospital uses to store patient records? I'll find out and this could lead to more information on what is going on. He heard his name called, the fictitious doctor that he was portraying, he immediately ran to the call. And then spent the next part of the remaining workday simply following orders. After what seemed to be the longest day yet and as tired and exhausted as he could be. Standing in the parking lot at his car, he looked down to see that his rear tire was flat.

Taking all of his might not to verbally express his true feeling at that moment, he breathed in then bent down, and counted to ten. Then reopened his eyes only to see that it was still there. He took off his coat, threw it in the backseat, and then got the spare out of the trunk and jack. He was down on his knees trying to change it out to the spare when he heard a car stop behind him. He instantly rose to stance and ready to run. To his relief it was the hospital security cart that maintains the parking lot. The man sitting behind the wheel of this cart, then asked him if he had a flat. Bond said yes, thinking that he was going to offer help. He looked at him and smiled. The man then asked him if he wanted him to call the AAA roadside assistance for him. He felt like just falling in overwhelming grief at that moment when he hears this reply.

He bent back down and said no thanks, then verbally said every expletive word in the vocabulary of mankind under his breath while he finished changing this flat. Now with the regular tire that went flat held up by him to place in the trunk, he saw a two-inch nail jammed into it sideways. He then wondered, was it planted there? He didn't drive by any work sights, but then again, there could be many reasons why a loose nail would be on the road. I only hoped. He sat behind the wheel of his car riddled with sweat and overwhelming tiredness, and then longed to just walk on the beach and hear the sounds of the shore. He put in reverse and left the parking lot laughing to himself, "I can walk around the swimming pool with the hairy dogs behind me." Now more familiar with the freeway traffic, he was thankful that for some reason that night it was light making the trip home all the easier.

Inside the house he walked right by Troy on his way to the bedroom. Troy noted this, and then walked following him and asks him, "What was wrong?" Bond responded, "The whole day and I have a flat tire that needs to be change. Can you call someone to fix it?" he threw him the keys, Troy caught them. He went back to the kitchen; both dogs looked up to him. "Well, dinner how do you two feel about a dog, ah a hot dog." Both of them wagged their tails. "Okay hot dogs, but first I need to make a call." They both whined. "Don't worry, five minutes, tops okay." They whined again. "Four minutes," they're now quiet. He smirked then called a mobile auto repair.

Troy went outside with his hot dog and dog food for the dogs, they still watched him to see if they were going to get any of what he was eating. Finished with the dog, he looked up seeing Bond come out. He offered him a hot dog, he shook his head no. "I just need to unwind," he then took a walk around the swimming pool, the dogs followed. Troy stayed there at the table with a bottle of beer waiting for Bonds' return seeing he was going to say anything.

Bond took three walks around the pool, then stood tense in motion and locked in an angered facial expression. The dogs ran from the pool area where he was. Troy thought of going to him to ask what was wrong, but then thought better of it. Instead, he took everything off of the patio table and went inside the house.

He sat in front of the TV and then heard of the latest corona virus outbreak, more than 20,000 people had contracted this horrendous disease there in Nevada, and the worldwide total and he turned off the TV before he could hear it, feeling defenseless at this time. Bond came inside while the dogs stayed outside. He walked to the couch and sat down; Troy looked at him, remaining silent. Bond then bit his lips and opened dialogue speaking with Troy.

"Let alone from the organ transfer that Horton is making in the hospital, I saw them at the hospital take a live person from the O.r. in a hidden room and I do not know what they were going to do with it next. I mean I saw it. They are playing God. We have to stop this. And we needed to do it yesterday." He got up then started leaving the room, then in one motion then in one moved him, returned to the couch. Troy breathed out speechless. Bond then got up and helped himself to a beer.

"Hopefully when I speak to Jonathan tomorrow, he'll know something," Troy was now too upset to return to his place for much-needed sleep. He again turned on the television and immediately flicked past the local and news stations and turned to a movie channel. The first one that he found he stopped at. It was just starting. He thought how appropriate, "The Cuckoo's nest." Bond stopped his movement and worry to watch it. "You've got to be kidding, hum Michael Douglas is in it, hum." He then seemed to calm himself to get lost in the movie, they both did.

When it ended, they watched all the credits to the very end, like a teenager that wanted to see all of her favorite rock stars concert at the very end. Troy turned it off, they both sat there unmoved and unspeaking for minutes until they got up and went their ways not even saying good night to each other. Troy looked up to the sky to try and see the moon, he couldn't find it. The misty streaked clouds adorned the overhead skies, something that he thought very odd, like something of a Halloween movie. "I had better get in my place before," he stopped to see the dogs but they were either invisible or not there. He thought while turning the knob to get into his casita, they were acting a bit strange, something that he never saw them behave like before. He closed and locked the door quickly behind him.

The following morning was hot, then a strong rain storm fell violently from the sky and lasted for around 15 minutes, they usually never lasted longer than 5 minutes. He got wet walking over to the main house. Inside the kitchen, coffee was brewed and two cups down from the overhead cabinets, but no Bond. He checked the hall, then his bedroom and the other room, no Bond. The front door then opened and Bond burst in. He saw the troubled look on Troy's face. "Relax, I just went for a morning run, and of all things in July it rains?" "It's Vegas, usually the rain doesn't last this long though, a bit odd."

"I'm going to go shower and change, help yourself to get some coffee." Troy did, he went against usually not drinking it, but then he thought everything now is a bit different. In taking the first sip he made a sour expression, then poured some milk in and he tolerated much better. He thought of scrambling some eggs, but then remembered how Bond rejected him the last time, so he toasted English Muffins instead. The dogs were now in the backyard, but instead of running and playing as they usually did, they were laying still seemingly just looking ahead to what, he could not tell.

Bond was there now pouring himself coffee, and then reaching for the milk to pour in it. "That was a quick shower. "Yeah, and I already knew what I wanted to wear, so that made it faster also." "It seems that you can't wait for this day to start." "Quite to the contrary, no but I want to get this job done." They each sit and have the muffins, putting orange marmalade on them. "It seems that Horton is the owner of the property that just exploded in the fire. Well, there was a large insurance policy also just taken out of it, claiming that it was an abandoned property. But had just been re-zoned for housing, increasing its market value." "He has led somewhere. How did he get that smart in jail?" "We are working against power here. And he lives in the Crystal towers." Troy almost choked on his toast. "You have to be a multimillionaire to live there, how?" "He does have assets that could lead in the wrong direction."

"Will you be going to the hospital today?" "No, too risky after the flat tire yesterday. I don't know if that was a message or not. But I am not going to risk it. I have to find out; we have to find out what Jonathan has found out if anything. I am a little surprised on no contact with him. Which means either he hasn't found out anything yet or it is too unsafe to get in touch with us so at this point I am waiting for him. I do not want to jeopardize anything that he has right now. right now, he is the next steppingstone in this plan."

"Is everything okay with your father and brother?" Bond sighs, then takes a deep breath, then takes his hand to his nose and lowers it down to his throat. "He says that the whole thing is alright, but what is not being said is what has me worried. Especially with Chris, the travel, (he breathes out and swallows), the whole thing, but I can't think about that right now. We have to be as calm as possible." Troy nods his head, and then says, "Spy School 101." Bond laughs, "You bought the program, ha?" They both laugh, and then get up from the table.

The next morning, Troy leaves for work. Once there he goes in through the gates after getting out of his jeep, he is happy to see that the lights are on in the office and the open sign is up. Inside, he gets a bit worried when he doesn't see Jonathan/Larry there. He hears footsteps approach from behind him, the door closes and here he is. "Good morning." Jonathan just nods his head. "There is a letter in the back that came for you here. I told you no personal mail at this address. Go check it out, and then get to work."

Troy responds yes, and then goes to find the letter. He picks it up, it is an envelope, it just has his name on it, and it was nothing from the actual official mail. It reads: Camera now on in the office watching the front desk. I did some exploring last night. Meet at Chicken Shack south rainbow, after work, Burn letter. Troy puts the letter inside his shirt, and then goes back to the counter where Jonathan stands posing as Larry. He is now wearing a face mask.

Once that he is face to face with him, he tells him to put on the mask. He hands him one and the first thing to do is drive the perimeter of the property as usual. Troy nods in response, puts on the mask and leaves to do this.

Driving the perimeter of the facility, he thinks another step taken and hopefully a big step. He had become very familiar with the workings of the operation there and also a bit bored, it was far different than being a movie double. The biggest thing that he did miss but too vain to admit it was the fame. Although he was not the lead actor, he still represented the actor and the accolades that came with the job. He prayed that this pandemic would soon be over and the world could go back to what it was even with all of the problems of daily life.

He was lost in flight as to what to do safely now. He just got in the car and drove around the east part of the valley hoping to see anything that could help him to solve this case.

At a stop light-waiting for the light to change, a certain van caught his eye. It was an ordinary commercial van that had the banner Phoenix enterprises on the side of it. It was in his right in the west direction waiting to make a right to the same direction that he was traveling. He then looked to where he was in these three lanes of traffic, that was stopped and waiting at the middle lane behind a Malibu and a plumbing truck. He hoped above God that they would not notice him.

He wore his dark glasses and lowered himself as much as he could in the car. He contemplated whether to try and follow it or to check out this apartment complex. He couldn't call Chris for backup as he usually did. The light turned green for him to go but the van was still stopped; at that point he had no choice but to go straight ahead with the flow of traffic. He looked to each side of the road, seeing what was there, was there any place that he could turn into and then quickly get out of in pursuit? Up a head past another stop light to the left was a McDonald with entrances and exits. He moved to the left lane and was honked at. He didn't have to apologize to the driver of this car; he just kept in motion and pulled into the lot, then parked instead of going forward to the drive thru.

He counted the passing seconds feeling his heartbeat faster as each one passed. He then thought that he should have parked further down in the lot as he was now on the side directly behind the drive thru waiting area. The enterprise van drove past this place; they had made the necessary left turn to get in there but drove on by. Bond was able to get out and turned out of the lot heading left to follow it. The amount of traffic greatly decreased making him far more visible, but at this time he wasn't thinking about that. It turned into a cyclone gated business complex with other enterprise trucks in the lot and one windowless two-story cement building. He drove right on by, knowing what he found out. The main thing now was to get out of there.

His drive turned out to be very informative. I found out two significant things. I'll go back to the other side of town now. Hopefully I will see her again; she doesn't pick up her cell. He stopped at the same place where he met her and got a cup of coffee. Other people were standing outside, making it impossible to wait there and keep social distance. He stood by his car leaning against it, he drank the coffee and still waited for 15 minutes after that. "No Laurie," he walked over to the trash can and threw his cup away.

Feeling broken-hearted he started the engine, put it in reverse then left the lot and headed home. He used the travel time to think of everything and how to plan the next step. "I miss Chris, in more ways than one."

Instead of going right back home, he checked out the Crystal apartment complex where Horton had earlier left. Now in front of it, he waited and parked to the side of the iron entrance gate. He watched as various people traveled in and out of this complex. They entered a code to get in; the problem with this is even if he knew the code there was a camera recording of all the traffic. You could drive right out though, if he left his car parked to the side of the entrance, which was in the welcomed shade. And it was out of the way of cars entering. Even if he jumped on the back of a truck, how could he just walk out?

"Dilemma now solved." He went to the back of his car and opened the trunk, then pulled out a leather gym bag. He took it behind one of the trees that was shading the area, and came back around to his car now dressed in a sweat suit.

He took the keys and locked the car. Then ran in circles to try at least to build up the breathing of exercise, while eyeing the vehicles driving to the gates. A delivery truck with a bottom steel hand latches perfectly. He times his run then ran behind it and as it stopped for the gate to open, he grabbed hold of the latch and made it through the gate. Once inside, he jumped off onto the pavement. He then ran to the tower. The front glass door was opened as someone was just leaving, he picked up the pace of a run, it seemed like he couldn't slow down. Now in front of the doors, people walking out held the door open for him to enter. Knowing that if the front gate was filmed the entrance, there was most likely filmed as well. He stopped his run, and then ran in place to ease his heartbeat as a runner would do. He then made his way to board on the side of the wall at the mailboxes. It gave the name and apartment number of each resident. He viewed which one was Horton's but after seeing this and then hearing increased voices, fearing one might be security he ran out never looking back. He jogged at the side of a car leaving the building on the way out and immediately went to his car with the keys already in hand, he started the engine then left.

Now back at the house, he parked in the garage and went inside hearing the dogs bark in the backyard. "Okay, okay, just wait a bit and I'll be out there with you." He used the bathroom then grabbed a bottle of water and went to go see them. He notices the loud sounds of birds and then saw quite a few of them in the yard. He went back inside with the dogs. "This time I'll feed you." He filled their bowls and put them down on the floor by the door to the backyard. "It is sure a lot cooler in here, bet you like that. I wonder what is wrong with those birds." He took off his shoes, and then sat in the easy chair. "Life at this moment somehow feels like a puzzle board that I have to put all the pieces in. I just worry what is going to happen when I get them all in there."

Not wanting to cook dinner and knowing that it was going to be at least an hour before anyone was home, he went into his room and took a nap. He was surprised at how he instantly fell asleep and for a brief time the world was silent.

# Chapter 34

MEETING OUTSIDE OF the back-parking lot of a Chicken Palace on the south side of town. They each held a sandwich and sodas inside Troy's jeep. "It was sure a long drive to get here."

"Exactly", Jonathan answers back without the mask of Larry. He still wore sunglasses and had a wide scarf around his neck with a baseball hat, "far from the storage area and far from his whereabouts." He takes a bite of the sandwich but hearing nothing in return Troy takes a bite as well.

"As you know of the short distance from the storage unit to the hospital, there are only those two buildings in between. Do you know what those two buildings are? Didn't you think it odd that they are both iron gates and that there is no entrance or exit to either building or no parking lot either?" "Maybe nobody has made note of this thinking that the building is closed due to the pandemic." "That is what I thought until I went to these gates, they are cemented shut, and there is no way to even open the gate unless it is blasted open." "You mean it is being protected?" "My thoughts, exactly, last night I took a little crawl." "Don't you mean walk?" "No crawl. I went back inside unit B, first disabling the monitor." "Wasn't that dangerous, I mean, if they couldn't see anything, whoever is watching it." "Way ahead of you, I put in a solid screen to feed the same picture of nothing while I was in there. All they saw was a barren inside of buildings," "Buildings, not building?"

"There is a tube system that runs from the storage unit through these buildings right to the hospital, surprise." "But how long would this take, I mean it is quite a distance." "It took 3.8 minutes." "How did you find this out?" "Oh, I am still dizzy. I rode it. Talk about a space rocket." "But Bond said that they were taking still, 'undead' bodies out of surgery and to a 'Special room'." "Yes, it depends on the need. When there is a higher demand and they don't have the 'needed ones, they get them'." "You mean to say, if they don't have enough of a specific organ, they kill someone to get it." Jonathan made no verbal reply, he just looked at him in a looked glare then looked down.

"Wow, how are we going to stop it?" "I have a few ideas, but I need to run them by Bond." "Now please tell me that you will tell him about this." Troy nods his head. Jonathan finished his last bite; he looks to Troy now hurriedly chewing. Jonathan gets out, and then Troy moves back to the driver seat, puts on his sunglasses and backs out of a lot to begin the journey back home. While driving listening to the music over the car radio and trying to calm him, he says aloud, "Undead bodies" then shivers.

# Chapter 35

CHRIS DROVE THE black SUV to a medical office complex. He parked, then took off his sunglasses and looked in the rear-view mirror. "It's me, right now anyway." He walked sure-footed to the rear side of the building then stopped looking at the door before opening it. "I feel nervous, unlike me." He paused, then opened the door and checked in with the receptionist then sat to wait to see the doctor. As his name was called from the now open door, he still felt a bit of reluctance in being there, but then pushed himself to go to the open door.

He followed this woman in the office and under his breath said, "hah, another door." She looked up to him and then introduced him to the female professionally dressed woman that sat behind the desk. She was mid-aged, brown hair pulled up and clipped, and wide glasses, white skin. He started to shake her hand, then remembered the current epidemic and just said hello and sat down. There were two chairs in front of her desk; he sat in the one on the right side.

"So, tell me why you are here?" "It didn't start until just recently…there are moments when I just, (he huffs) lose it and I don't know why." "When you say lose it, what do you mean by that? What you doing?" "Nothing specific-what scares me, is my wife." "Your wife scares you? Has she always made you feel this way?" "No, you see we just got back together. I was away for a long time, and she thought that I was dead." "When you say dead, do you mean as physically dead?" he pauses, then looks down to his feet.

The doctor picks up on this. "There is no one here but you and I, and what you say are strictly confidential, between us."

"I had to be dead or have her and everyone else thinks that I was dead as part of the job." She stops looking like she was going to say something, and then remained silent for him to proceed. "Well, the job was finished and we reunited, the classic love story then things just started falling apart. She would go through mood swings and I tried to deal with her and calm her then all of a sudden I," he fidgets, "I don't want to talk about it anymore, I have already said too much." He gets up to leave.

"Look, I am only here to help you. I have listened to just a, what I think is a very small amount of what is bothering you. I am only here to help you. I have open ears and no judgment." He stops, then turns to her and replies, "I don't know what to do, and that is not me, not me at all." "And this is why you are here, sit." He does and he goes on to tell her more of his present problems. She asked him if his wife is going through the change. He tells her that he doesn't think so. She listens more to him.

"Your wife is going through grief. This is a very complicated thing, denial (he shakes his head), anger (shakes his head), bargaining, depression (he shakes his head), and acceptance." He looks at her in question. "Maybe, she should come here." "No, I don't want her to know." "You don't want her to know, but are you here for her or you?" "Me." "You are experiencing, PTSD." "No, I am not."

"Okay, let me ask you some questions, they are all an easy answer, ready?" he nods his head. "Have you ever experienced a traumatic event in your life?" he lifts his head and retracts his lips giving no verbal answer. Are you experiencing, flashbacks?" he gives the same response. "Are you having upsetting dreams or nightmares on these events?" "Trouble sleeping," "Are you avoiding people's places or activities? Do you have negative thoughts about yourself?" "Please, please just stop...the answer is yes to all of the above, is YES, IT JUST STARTED!"

The doctor smiles to him, "You sir, have come to the right place. I want to see you next week, I can help." He looked calm hearing her response. She writes him a prescription. He takes it from her and asks her what it is.

"It is a prescription for Zoloft, this will help you. Go over everything with the pharmacist- you Chris, are doing the right thing. Thank you for coming here today, see you next week." He gets up feeling a sort of relief, feeling glad that he finally made the step to go there.

He takes the prescription to his regular pharmacist then does wait to talk with him in the correct use of this medication. Now in the car, he just doesn't feel like going home yet. With the current lockdown, going almost anywhere will most likely be closed. Maybe just a drive, after a few miles up the road, he parks and puts on his face mask then goes inside a deli for a takeout order. He goes back to his SUV with a bottle of Pellegrino and a ham sandwich, mayo, and lettuce only, just like he likes. He eats it in the car seeing no other option and watches traffic go by.

Getting out of the SUV at another medical building, he has trouble walking through the parking lot to the main building from the sun rays in his eyes as he had left his sunglasses in the car. He did have his face cover on. Inside his doctor's office in the exam room, he was happy to hear his long-time elderly male doctor tell him that he checked out good. Although his blood pressure was a little on the high side, his doctor then asked him about his diet and if he had any stress in his life. He flatly responded to the stress of the worry of the pandemic, which seemed to satisfy the doctor.

The doctor left, the nurse then gave him a COVID 19 test. They swab up the nose, he was worried about it, felt odd for only a brief moment, and then it was over. He was then informed that he would get the results later. He wasn't worried about it though; he mostly just took the test as a precaution. On his way back to the parking lot, he thought of his daughter and he hoped that she was safe from this virus. He made a mental note to call her tonight.

Now driving, he felt sad, being that he had missed so much of his daughter's life and watching her grows. Then he thought well her kids. I am too young to be a grandfather. He then thought, is it really this point in my life? Well, younger people than me are grandparents. Where did everything go? I was working… just get home to…my family.

Driving into the estate, he felt warmth go through his body. Home, it was always there like a rock. The feeling that he didn't like. He was going into it and hearing only silence: sometimes silence was welcome, but now right then and there he felt a feeling of fear. He silently and carefully maneuvered himself through the landscape of the house. He didn't find Jane, which in itself was disturbing. And his father was not in his office. Very carefully, silently and slowly he opened the door to his father's bedroom. Vincent was laid on his bed. Chris ran to him and lifted his wrist, feeling for a pulse.

"I am alive, just tired." "Where is Maggie?" "Maggie, ah, she drove your wife to the doctor." "To the doctor, (fear ran down his spine) what is wrong?" "She said that she needed to see, ah, something about what Bond had told her." "My brother, what is he doing talking to her on her about health?" "Don't worry…I'm sorry, but I…am… tired." He closed his eyes to sleep. Chris once more held up his wrist to feel a pulse. Feeling it, he gently laid it back down to his body. "I think that I am going to call my brother."

Chris again checked all of the houses for her, she wasn't there. "It is not a good idea for a father to be alone, we don't even have the cook or mechanic anymore." He walks in circles then goes outside to the backyard and listens for the sound of the waves. "It is like they are non-existent today; I don't hear them." He paces back and forth, and then goes back into the house. Let's see its 2:00 here, so in Vegas, it is evening or night.

Jesus, Bond what did you tell her?" he goes to their bedroom and still looks for her; he picks up her sweater from the top of the dresser, sits on the edge of the bed and holds it then smells it. Yes, it is her. Please, please be okay. He dials Bond's cell number, nervously waiting for an answer. In a very tired voice, he hears his brother say hello. "What is the matter, are you okay?" Bond says yes. "You don't sound like it." "I had a long day and I am just tired." "Is anybody else there with you?" "I don't know, I am in the bedroom asleep." "You just don't sound right." "I, ah, ah," "I am going to call Jonathan." "No, no (his voice springs up) you can't call him, he is not him." "What?"

Bond tried getting out of the bed but feels exhausted and weak. He starts to roll out then captures himself on the very edge with his legs fleeing for the floor. "Bond, Bond! Are you alright?" In sleepy motion, he captures the phone and leans his mouth to it. "Just tired, I told you, can I talk to you later?" The phone then goes dead. "My God, I hope that is alright and he is just tired. I know that it is Vegas, but the lockdown. He doesn't have the virus, does he? And why can't I call Jonathan? What is the other guy's name?"

"Where is my wife?" he tries calling her cell phone, there is no answer. "God, what has happened to her?" he runs down the stairs as hearing voices from the doorway. Both she and Maggie are there. Maggie says hello, then leaves to check on Vincent. She looks at him and smiles. "What, where were you?" She stands back from him and he can tell that she doesn't want to say anything. "I am your husband and I worry, just please tell me."

"Maybe we had better go sit down and I'll tell you," He more than worrying after hearing this, walked to the couch and sat down beside her. She breathed in then rocked her body forward, then sat back. "I know that I have been feeling a bit different lately." He opens his eyes wide fearing what she is going to say. "Your brother told me about grief. I denied it, because it just sounded so simple, but after seeing the doctor today about it." Chris felt his body just lose all of the built-up tension at that point. He hugged her. "I haven't even finished telling you about this." He thought of apologizing then just listened to her instead. He paid very close attention to everything that she did say and he then told her of his experience with the doctor. It was like a weight had been lifted off of each one of them.

They hugged.

# Chapter 36

FEELING HIS BODY ache with tissue in hand because of a runny nose, he holds the wall trying to make it down the hallway to the kitchen. "One moment I am burning hot and the next I feel chills going all through my body, oh God," he grabs the wall trying to make it to the trash can in time to throw up. Another second and he would have missed it. "I feel like I have to throw up but hardly anything come out. I just need to make it to the sink for a glass of water." He gets there leaning on the side of the counter the entire way there. "I am so thirsty but I can only swallow a little bit. Oh God, it is hard to breathe." He swallows a cough and looks like he is much disoriented. An aspirin, he opens the cabinet and sees the only acetaminophen and takes that. "I feel hungry, but at the same time, I feel like I am going to throw up. I just need it, too. I am so tired." He makes it to the couch, and then lies down.

Troy walks in the house, the dogs fly out the door to the backyard. In walking forward, he hits a dog dish. Bond hears this and grudgingly says that he has already fed them. Troy walks over to him and then asks him what is wrong. After he is finished explaining his sickness, Troy moves back. Bond sees this then asks him what is wrong. "Brother, you have the virus." "What?" "Have you been taking precautions? Have you been wearing your mask?" Bond thinks about that question and truthfully answers back, "Twice." "In all of this time, you have only worn it twice?" "I wouldn't get it." "You've got it."

"It's too late to take you to the doctor right now." Bond whimpers in pain. "have you taken anything for it, the pain, anything?" "All that was in the cabinet as acetaminophen, that and water." "Good, that is what you can have." Bond can see Troy stand away from him and lift his head to the ceiling saying, "Oh, God.. I didn't get this on purpose." "I know, it is just what are we going to do about this case now?" Bond quietly moans. "I can't call Jonathan." He paces the room. "Oh, God," he stops his pacing then stands six feet from Bond, "I know that you didn't do this, it just proves how vulnerable we all are to this horrid disease. Christ. This is just going to wait until the morning. I am sorry Bond, but this is all that I know, maybe? Give me a moment." Troy goes outside and uses his cell phone. Fifteen minutes later he goes back into the house and sees that Bond looks like he is drifting in and out of sleep. "I found a clinic somewhat near here, where I can take you to get tested, then we'll know for sure" he hears Bond say, no. "I know that you are only saying no because you don't want anyone to know that you are here, but I highly doubt that Horton is checking medical office records." He puts his face mask back on then puts on the gloves from the kitchen sink and helps him up then gets him in the Mustang and drives him to the clinic.

Troy fills out the papers for him, pays then waits, standing up and watching Bond. He is called in; the nurse does his test in the hallway. A cotton swab in the nostril, she explains to Troy that it does look like he has the virus. There will be a short wait time to know the results, but until then stay home and drink water, and rest and stay away from people. Most importantly, above all shelter at home.

Troy takes him back home and then moves him to the master bedroom where he does not have to climb in and out of bed and the bathroom is right there connected to it. He stayed to make sure that Bond knew where he was and tracks for him to do if he quickly needed to get to the bathroom. It has been just ten steps and there is the bathroom. He stayed in the house for a while just to make sure that he was okay. In watching the television news, he could not imagine feeling worse. Instead of people coming together for the cause and just following these few simple rules: of shelter in place, face masks, 6-foot distance but they were protesting and vandalizing and picketing the police.

If someone is attacking you, raping you, stealing from you, and there are no police there, who are you going to call? Ghostbusters, I mean come on people God gave you a brain, use it. This is not the way to get your 5 minutes of fame. He turned the television off and didn't even look for an alternative channel. God, what are we going to do? How many more innocent people are going to disappear and die in the hospital? This turned out to be much more than I bargained for.

I wonder if he'll be alright for the night. I am a building away. He did leave only to come back 10 minutes later with his night clothes, toothbrush, etc. I guess that I'll be sleeping on the couch tonight. Maybe a little TV after all. He put in a DVD of Ghostbusters, and as he slid it in the player he replied, "What the hell, might as well watch it. I just hope that I can sleep tonight, I have no idea what tomorrow we'll bring." He was well into watching the movie and laughing and momentarily freeing himself, and then he heard a moan. He stopped the movie, then immediately went to check on Bond. He was burning with fever. Troy went back in the kitchen and dampened two towels with cold water, then took them back to Bond tossing them to the bed, maintaining distance. Bond thanked him. "Sorry, but I don't have a cure for you. I wish I did the whole world wishes that I did. I am sorry, but I am going to leave, I can't get sick. I am staying here tonight. I'll be in the living room on the couch, you are not alone." He stood back and told him to get better, then closed the door. He went back to the living room and turned the movie back on. Sitting in the easy chair he remarked, "I just don't know what else to do, both for him and the medical mystery." He then got up again hearing the dogs bark, he opened the door, and they both ran in the house. He looked into the backyard and saw a bird fall directly to the ground. "This is weird, like something out of an Alfred Hitchcock movie. I just don't want to go and pick that dead thing up, but the dogs." He went into the garage and got an empty box, then placed over the dead bird, cringing as he looked at it. "What is happening?" he went back inside and finished watching this movie with the dogs. They both lay on the couch. "Ah, you two, tonight that couch is mine." They then each whined.

The following morning the gardeners were there earlier than usual due to the extreme heat that the valley was feeling, the night before the cool down was only to 93 degrees, and the high was 114, today it will still be 111. Chris asked the gardeners who were regulars, he told them of the bird problem. A quick explanation was given that a group of ravens had come there and they were fighting with themselves for superiority. He raced back in the house already feeling the extreme heat of the day; it was already in the 90's." I got here just in time." He answered the front door, it was the movers there to take the parked truck out of the driveway, the one that blocked Bond's first bedroom.

After everyone was gone and he made one more check on Bond, who was now able to get out of bed then he left for work. In pajamas and bathrobe Bond left the bedroom, grabbed a glass of water, then sat down and turned on a morning talk show. "What is this guy's real name? They keep on referring to him as Jase." After three more mornings of watching this show that he became glued to and he found out his name was Jason feinberg and he had two cats. He was now a week into experiencing this virus and was getting more than restless. Later that afternoon, he showered and dressed then went to the kitchen drawer to pull out the car keys and found no keys, just a note. The note reads, "The keys are not here and you are quarantined, remember."

As he plunked himself back down in the chair in front of the television, "They know me." He breathed out, and then said, "Yeah, I never thought that I would get it in the first place, and now look at me. What is going on in the fight that I am here to stop?" he sighed deeply, "It is sure a lot different, to work without Chris. I hope that he is alright." He thought of texting him but then he thought, no news is good news.

He brought the dogs in the house that instantly laid on the couch, smiled to them, then got out a box of saltines and began nibbling on them. The dogs whined; he held the cracker up in the air and looked at it then the dogs. "I don't think that this is part of a dog's diet." He got up to get them Milk bones instead. He sat back down to the television looking at them munching away, then smiled. "I guess that I can get lost in a soap opera. Today will it be The Young and the restless or General hospital? Both."

# Chapter 37

CHRIS SPOKE WITH the psychiatrist, more at ease in every session. He, he was still on the medicine, he found that it helped.

He nervously mentioned something to the doctor regarding Jane and what he was going to have to do. She warned him of the consequences of doing this. It was something that he did not want to hear, but he knew that her case was right. He ended the session with both happiness and apprehension. Upon arriving home inside, he could see her through the living room window. She was outside painting. He first thought of going to her, but then thought differently, she was now at ease. Maggie was in the kitchen cooking something that did smell good. They each expressed a hello to each other. In not seeing his dad there, he went to check on him in his bedroom. He wasn't in the bedroom or bathroom. He was presently surprised at seeing him at his desk, he noticed him standing watching him and briefly smiled, looking up to him then right back down to his work. This made Chris happy. He then went to his bedroom, opened the closet and took out a shoe box. He sat there, sitting on the bed and just looked at the shoes and then heard his wife entering the room. He closed the box and put it back in the closet. Then turned to her and they embraced in a hug. She began telling him of her latest painting. He smiled to her glad that she was now in a good mood.

"It is almost dinner, let's go outside and take a walk to relax." "But I was just out there." "Not with me." They laughed then went outside for a walk on the beach. She could tell that he wanted to say something to her, but then each time he didn't. She then broke the silence. And told him about how to see had gotten much better, he smiled to her and told her that he could tell. They thought over and over again of not saying what he felt that he needed to say to her and remained silent thinking it's the only present option.

Dinner that evening was spaghetti and meatballs with garlic bread and broccoli salad. The talk of the evening was almost none as they were so transfixed in eating. After dinner they each went their separate ways. Things were returning to normal. The following morning everyone there was in their rightful place with the exception of Chris. Jane asked Vincent where he was, he gave her no answer. Looking through their bedroom again, she found a note that he had written on the side table.

"Jane, I have to go and take care of something, I'll only be gone for a little while, and do not worry I will be safe. You stay at home; family is there, love Chris." She was confused by it and wondered if it was an old note. She read it again and again, and then checked the closet and some of his things were gone. "Where did he go? I thought that everything was good between us, we were working so hard and now he just leaves…?" With the absence of Bond to confide to she sought out the only other person there to express her feelings to and that was Vincent. He listened to her, but offered her no answer. She didn't know if he was covering up for Chris in whatever dangerous thing that he was now involved in or if it was true and he simply did not know. She left Vincent's office and went back to the living room, stopped there and looked out of the increased current on the beach. "Everything is returning to normal, alright." She then sighed heavily.

Chris waited in his parked car in the parking lot of a shopping mall. He fidgeted with the radio dial to different stations, and then turned it off hearing nothing that he liked. A box was then brought out to him; he lifted back up his face mask, then signed for it and placed it in the backseat. Driving out of the parking lot he thought, well one thing done with. He drove about 40 more minutes then parked in an even larger parking lot.

He opened the box, then put the clothes in a leather suitcase, then took inventory of what he needed, then locked the car and left walking to an even larger building bypassing many, many cars.

Once inside this building, he stopped out of the way of foot traffic and turned his wedding ring then took a brief moment just to look at it. Looking to his right then to his left, he saw the route that he needed to go while saying in this mind, everything will turn out good for us, all of us. His walk turned into a run picking up his pace to get where he needed to go.

Back at the estate, Jane moved swiftly through all of the grounds, looking for any sign of him or clue to where he went and why. At the front of the house feeling her body collapse where she stood, she knelt to the ground in tears. "I am living a nightmare, please; please let me only be dreaming." She went back inside the house only to find it empty of him. Now, upstairs in their bedroom, she circles it and said, "What have I missed? He didn't say anything." lifting her hand to her head feeling only defeat, she has to find something, anything else. She opened drawer after drawer, then went through the closet thoroughly even the bathroom, then came back out to the bedroom holding nothing.

"Wait, what is that on the floor under the table?" She picks up and reads it, "A pamphlet talking about Singapore. Singapore, why?" feeling utterly lost, she holds it tighter with her arms and hands shaking, she can read scribbling in his handwriting on it. Flight 220 leaving Thursday at noon, she lowers it, closes her eyes and lowers it to her waist with her trembling fingers. Opening her eyes, she cries out, "Thursday, that is today. Maybe I can still make it there and go with him, meet him or just ask him why?"

Jane runs to her cell phone, picks it up and checks the time. Seeing it, she blinks, then looks again, and then falls into the chair. "Right now, it is 11:47 a.m., I would have to be Batman to make it there." She sniffs her nose then wipes tears from her eyes with a tissue. Then leans back in the chair, "No, I would have to be Superman; I think he is faster than Batman." She leaves the room going downstairs to talk to Vincent, as he is the only one here, and he doesn't know anything. "God, Bond, I miss you, you were my salvation. I just hope that you are okay and not meeting him there, for whatever reason."

She goes back upstairs to her laptop and Google's information on Singapore. "It seems that at first COVID19 passed by them, and then it attacked the poor underpaid workers there, where one toilet was shared by 15 people. The country takes great pride in itself, jaywalking taboo and there are government controls on virtually everything. Singapore is known for its tight surveillance. All schools, most businesses and even some doctor's offices are closed, masks are mandatory and shopping is only permitted for absolute necessities like food or medicine. Singapore is now divided into two cities, two populations: the foreign workers in dormitories, and the rest of us."

"If this is the way that it is, the outbreak is so bad, why on earth is he going there, for what reason? It was known as Utopia there, the operative word being 'was'. Why didn't he talk to me on this, I am his wife, right now, I do not feel like I am, though. I was working so hard on everything, and I thought that he was too. Oh God, what do I do now? Sit home and watch soap operas that are repeats of a long time ago…I guess, that is all that there is."

She turns on the television gets comfortable in the chair, then flicks the stations until she finds one that interests her and starts watching it. "And there isn't more. I can already feel like I am going to gain 15 pounds living like this. Already, I want popcorn." He gets up and takes out an energy bar from her purse, then sits down munching on it, "I can't believe that Vincent doesn't know. right now, I feel like a con or a stooge."

# Chapter 38

SITTING IN TERMINAL 9, Chris checks his phone at the time in Singapore, then hears the announcement that they are now boarding section A, which he is part of. He turns off his phone and boards the flight, sitting at the window seat in the first-class section feeling very happy that no one sits on the side of him or behind him. Now, seated, he turned his phone off. The takeoff was a bit bumpy at first gaining altitude but he had experienced a lot worse. The stewardess walked down the aisle checking on everyone. He closed his eyes to slumber just as the flight began.

He was awakened two hours later hearing the overhead announcement that bottled water and peanut packages were being served. He declined instead having water that he purchased in the gift shop of the airport-past security so they let it his take on. He more than felt that he was doing the right thing, the only difference was this time the family knew nothing about it.

To calm his questioning mind, he reverted to the principles that he learned in Judo classes. Utilize physical and mental strength most effectively; understand life through mental and physical training, and to develop one's self as a person to be useful to society. He then said softly aloud, "Balance." The stewardess came to him and asked him if he wanted anything, he smiled and shook his "no" and she left.

The arrival came more quickly than he thought, he was very glad that he did not feel tired as a person sometimes is after a long flight. Leaving the terminal gate, he saw Geishas waiting for a party with lies in their hands. He thought I was here as he walked around them, and then looked for the baggage claim area. He spotted his Prada leather trolley, sooner than expected. He grabbed it, and then went to the limo waiting area. Once he walked out of the glass sliding doors to this area, he thought of being a mark. He tipped his head to an attendant there, and then heard where he could get a private car to take him to the hotel instead. He did that, as usual, there was a wait, but not nearly as long as the wait for a taxicab.

Arrived at the hotel he went to self-check-in, there was a brief time of only 10 minutes and he had his room key card. He cautiously looked around him sweeping the perimeter thinking it too easy and fearing something. He went to his room, unpacked, showered, and changed into a sweatsuit that he just purchased. It fit better than he expected. Lastly, before he left, he changed into the new shoes he brought with him, Tommy Hilfiger Randal tennis shoes. After he left the room, now down to the main floor of the hotel, he went to the bar and got a Grey Goose Martini, then sat by the window looking out to the flowered garden.

# Chapter 39

AWARE OF THE feelings that Jane must be experiencing, Vincent's thoughts were to get back to the way that things used to be for himself and her. He brushed up on trivia knowledge, and then sat at the dining room table with water and snacks there waiting for her to make an appearance. After only a fifteen-minute wait, she showed up and smiled at him. She looked to him, then cleared her throat and asked him, "Was the Mona Lisa ever stolen?" he smiled tilted his head, then replied to her, "Yes, it was stolen in 1911; they considered that Pablo Picasso was the suspect but then later proved that an Italian handyman stole it. He went by the name of Vincenzo Perugia. It was recovered inside his hotel room in Florence. He took it out of the museum on a night that it was closed.

And also, Leonardo wrote backward. He was trying to prevent smudging. Writing left to right was too messy. The ink that he just put down would smear as his hand moved across it." She listened to him wide-eyed at this information that he gave her. When he finished, she paused in silence, then said to him, "Well, you got that one right." He then asked her to name the two explorers that claimed to have discovered the North Pole. Without hesitation, she replied, "Robert Perry" then only silence came from her mouth. He waited, then asked her, "And?" She looked to him on the question. "And name the other one." She looked to the door of the kitchen, then in pondered thought she replied, "Cook." He nodded, "You got that right, Fredrick Cook." She was now elated with herself.

At that time in trying to reach for anything of knowledge, she just couldn't seem to find it. She did then ask him, "Can a cat be allergic to humans?" he placed his hand over his chin, then ran it down his neck and replied to her "Yes." "You got that one right." "Who was the first president to be inaugurated in Washington D.C.?" She wiped her tongue over her lips then bit down lightly and swallowed. "John Adams." "No," She fidgeted in the chair, "it was Thomas Jefferson." She then bolted up from the chair and started leaving the room. "Where are you going?" "To think of more questions to stump you," he smiled watching her leave. At least now one important thing is returning to normal.

His cell phone rang; he picked it up off of the table and answered. "Bond, it is good to hear from you but is something wrong?" Bond explained to him that he indeed had the virus, upon hearing this from Bond, Vincent said a silent hail Mary and moved his hand in the air in the direction of making a cross. "How is Chris? I could sure use him here." Vincent sidestepped around this question and told him that Jane was doing much better. Bond breathed out after hearing this. He knew that his father did not want to give him the answer to this question. They made small talk for a bit, and then Bond swallowed hard on the phone and again asked his dad where Chris was. Vincent looked down at the table, and then knew that there was no way for him to dodge this question asked by his son. "Chris, well he is…" "He is where?" "He left Jane a note before he left." "Okay, so she knows now I need to know, where?" "Singapore." "Singapore? By himself, why, whatever for? How is this helping us solve this case?"

Vincent then shifted his face to show no emotion, "You know your brother; he must have a good reason." Bond paused, looking only at dead air, feeling trapped within him. "Yeah, well you take care father." "I love you son." Bond hung up.

After taking a few minutes to calm himself, he got up then sat at the kitchen table opening his laptop and started googling information on Singapore. After reading only two stories he found out that Singapore was once considered a Utopia. And virtually crime-free, basically everyone followed the rules, jaywalking was even against the law. The plague had first passed them by now they too, as the rest of the world are riddled with it. In the poor working class, there was a dramatic surge in this infection. "Chris, why are you going there? Is there a tie to Horton there somewhere?

Only you know." He leaned his head in his lap and moaned in pain. "I had better get back to bed, I am so hot and feeling dizzy." He got up then went to the kitchen counter to lean against it then thought of more Acetaminophen. "No, I just took some a few hours ago." He gets a towel then took it to bed and laid it on his head once rested. "When will this ever, pass?" he turned to each side then lay still with the towel over his forehead. "Chris, I only hope that you are okay and doing the right thing."

# Chapter 40

BACK IN THE hotel room, he opened his laptop and connected it to the Wi-fi, then he grabbed a rice bowl out of a brown paper bag that he brought up from the bar. He pressed a few buttons on the computer, and then took a bite from the chicken rice bowl. "Let's see epoch Times news." He stirred it, then pierced a large piece of chicken and took it to his mouth. Now chewing it, he logged on to a story.

"When the Plague arrives by the epoch Times-News Staff," It went back in history explaining the different plagues, Nero executed Christians. rome's great mistake was to persecute Christianity. He asked, "What is our greatest mistake today? When rulers become corrupt, natural disasters will happen." He then asked, "Why now and why us? There is a turning point. Powerful empires were brought to their knees by plagues. Right now, people are trapped in China. And right now, there are Concentration Camps in China, where citizens are killed for their organs. The police are taking people off of the street for no reason and they are being sent there and killed for their organs. The organs are being sold on the foreign transplant market."

As he finished reading this story, he put down the plastic fork and paused in silence. "Bond said that with this we are playing God. What is happening here is humanity is playing the devil. How is this happening, and all for money and power, not for humanity?" he got up then in a brisk pace walking circles the room. "Father, what did you get us involved in?" he picked up his pace even more then came to an abrupt stop. "You got us involved in today, the problems of today. Why hasn't our President told us the American public anything about this? It is happening and there is a black market for it." He again began circling the room, then waved his hands up in the air and swiped through the air hitting nothing, then fell to the bed. "This is the world that my daughter is growing up in." He sat up sighed, then closed his eyes and re-opened them. "I am going to make a sure-footed step in making a change…I don't know if I am in the right place at the right time, but it feels like it." He cradles his back, then sways back and forth and stands up looking to the blank canvas of the life ahead of him. "I am the master of my fate and I will do well." He goes back to the table, sits then looks at the food box in front of him. "Father, Bond, Jane, Lauren, I hope and pray that you are all okay. Okay for now and for the future." He waited to capture everything that he just said, then went back to eat the food looking out of the hotel room window and hearing a jet plane fly by. "I know, I will get back as soon as I can." He closed his eyes, then the food box and placed it back inside the bag it came in then spoke in soft words, "I miss you, now and forever."

Throwing the bag in the small trash container he remarked, "This, I should have started yesterday."

Bond rested and now feeling a little better, he got up went to the bathroom then splashed water on his face not even looking in the mirror. "Something I don't know what it is, but something does not feel right." He left the bathroom then made it back to the hall now be able to walk down it not holding on to the side walls. He looked out the side window of the front door and watched some neighbors get out of his car and go inside his house. "It is funny, I have been here it feels like for a very long time, but

I do not even know who they are, but does it matter. We are all equals." He sits down, and then turns on the television. The news is on, he listens. "Today the number of deaths and reported cases of the Corona virus in Nevada has reached an all-time high, folks, we are now in the red zone." After hearing this, he turned the television off then got up and went to the kitchen sink. He swallowed water with ease not having the trouble that he had before. He looked thankful for this. He stood there at that moment, being and feeling dormant in what to do. Looking out the window, he saw the dogs looking up to him as he stood looking out the window. "Okay, you two, your food are coming." He fixed them each a bowl then brought it outside to them. Then he stayed outside sitting at the patio table. The larger one looked at him, then stopped her eating and went over to him and put her head at his hand. He smiled and petted her. "You are happy and I am glad of that. Now go back and eat your food." She lifted her head back up to him, and then went back to her food bowl.

"I don't even know your names. When Troy gets here, I'll ask him. I haven't even heard him call you two by your names. Or maybe it's just dog one and dog two." He laughed after saying this. He then heard his car in the long side driveway. Troy came inside the gate and looked very concerned about seeing Bond outside. He walked up to the side of him not getting to close and asked him, "Shouldn't you be inside resting?" "Oh, I have done nothing but rest, it is getting rather boring." "Still, I think that you or we should go inside, come on." He opened the door and then stood back for Bond to enter the house.

Troy took a beer from the refrigerator then twisted off the cap and took a swig. He looked at Bond sitting at the table watching him. "Sorry, but you can't." "Hey, don't feel bad for me. I could never drink one the way I feel now anyway." "Sorry, that bad still, ha?" "Oh, right now better, but earlier, it comes, and it goes. I just wish that it would go away permanently." "Yes, I wish that for you too." "How did it go today at work?" he breathed out, "long and boring, it seems at this moment we are just trapped." Bond rose up his facial expression in deep concern. "What do you mean trapped?" "Oh, relax, everything is going as a typical workday would, it is just that we haven't stopped anything yet. I don't know if Jonathan is waiting for more information to do something- he hasn't told me. I am just doing nothing but work there." Bond shook his head. "Yeah, that is hard. But maybe no (at this point Troy jumped in and talked with him) no news is good news." They laughed and right at that moment the dogs each let out one bark each.

The front doorbell rang. Bond jumped, then saw Troy walk calmly to the door lookout then open it. Bond relaxed. Troy came back in with a pizza. He placed it on the table and apologized to Bond about it. Bond said that it sure smelled good and that he was going to try a slice. They both enjoyed the Pepperoni pizza. Troy was glad to see Bond eat and Bond was glad that he was able to.

Jonathan checked his latest text message, and then quickly deleted it as he stood in the back room where his residence is at the storage office. A slight smile momentarily came to his face. He went back to the office and turned off all of the necessary lights, then turned the alarm on. Leaving the bathroom now dressed in his pajamas, he picked up a book from the nightstand, and then got in the twin size bed against the wall. "It looks like it is just you and me tonight, Dean." He opened, put on his reading glasses and made himself comfortable in the bed.

The next morning at the storage office, Jonathan went through all of the customary procedures to open the business. He had even gotten to know some of the customers by their names. He continuously looked at his wristwatch. Hearing the sound of the bells signifying that the door was being opened, he looked up to Troy and verbally said aloud, "You are late." He said he was sorry but he had gotten a late start.

Jonathan answered the gate box. He looked at the security cameras and saw a white Chevy van stopped at the gate. The voice that came from his desk speaker responded that he was from the alarm company, and he was there to check to the system. Jonathan replied back to him, "Yes, I read your text yesterday that you were coming today." He pressed for the gate to open for him to drive in. Troy looked up to him in question; he saw this then acted bothered by it as Larry would have. "Just go to work, everything is fine." Troy went out the door right to the Cushman and took his usual morning drive around the perimeter of the grounds.

The man from the truck drove right to the side of the office while parked they went inside to talk with Larry, after just a few moments this man left the office with keys to all the units. Troy saw this and thought it a bit odd but then Jonathan told him everything was good. The van stopped at the side of unit B. Troy again thought it odd that it didn't start at unit A. Was this man working for Horton Baxter? He thought of texting Bond regarding it but then thought that he'd just wait until there was a need to.

Watching him get out of the van, he noticed that this man, he definitely had a leg limp, and also blonde dreadlocks coming from his white baseball cap and his arms were very tan. Too much time had gone by that he was just sitting here watching him so he started back driving around the area. This man that gave his name as Tom to Larry opened the lock of the backside of the B Unit and went right to the light switch like he already had knowledge of the building layout. He entered the building and closed the door behind him. Back in the office, Larry saw that the large Phoenix Van was at the gate waiting for it to open.

Larry was uptight and nervous as he looked to the screen that showed this white van in front of unit B and no sign of Tom. The enterprise van now drove in, and there was no sign of Tom. Larry hit the button that sounded the alarm bell, and then turned it off in only a minute. He did see that the Phoenix van stopped while this happened. He looked back to the unit B camera and saw the white van now gone. He circled all of the TV screens showing the property and didn't see it, where did it go?

The enterprise van, now parked exactly where the white van has earlier been. He saw Horton and his guard, get out and go to the door. They opened it, and then stepped back. Larry thought, oh no, why and what. He then found that they opened the back of the large van that blocked the camera and were there for their usual 30 minutes. Before leaving they stopped at the office and informed him that the inside lights of the building were hot and they wanted to know why. Without hesitation, Larry replied that the light bulbs were just changed as quarterly maintenance. Horton then told him that they would take care of these themselves and there was no need to go into the unit. Larry nodded his head to him as they left the office and drove out.

Troy went into the office; Larry looked at him wanting to hear anything from him as to the news of what happened. Troy placed the company keys to him on the counter. "I found this right under the bush at the side door of the office, did you drop them?" Larry took them then said thank you. At this point, there was so much unmasked in not answering this question correctly. "Since you got here late today, I am going to take an early lunch." He looked back to the counter, and then yelled out to Troy before he exited the room. "I feel like a little air now, I'll take a drive around the property." Troy handed him the keys to the Cushman and he left.

Driving around the property, he drove by unit B first just observing it but making no stop. At unit A, he stopped focusing on one of the larger units. Visually looking at the rope swing that came out from the bottom of the unit the combination lock was unlocked. He took it off then grabbed hold of the rope and viewed the inside of this unit. He raised his eyes to what he saw then rolled the door back down and left it unlocked then drove back to the office.

Troy looked up to him, and then made his way from behind the counter for Larry to return to standing behind the counter. "I won't be taking that early lunch, after all units A 32, has just been rented out. It's not locked by the owner as he is coming back today." Troy nodded his head then left. Larry entered that unit filled on the computer. "Just a typical working day," he then huffed in boredom.

# Chapter 41

THE EMERGENCY CORRIDOR of the hospital was busy, crying sounds from the waiting room. Sure, footed doctors walking into various rooms and taking clipboards as the computers had become overwhelmed. A new set of footprints roamed these hallways, and he was most welcomed being a doctor. He had brownish-gray wavy hair, tall mid-build glasses and already admired by many nurses there. He was approached by a nurse ready to assign him to a newly admitted patient. "I can't, I am already late to the O.r." She quickly stepped back.

In the elevator to the downstairs operating rooms, three other white coated men were in there. Right before the doors opened, the older one of these men looked at him, then said to him, "Jensen, good I need you now, follow me to scrub for my next surgery. I may not need you, but I'll tell you more as we scrub." He nodded, then scrubbed with the doctor and went to the O.r. with him. It was a long and complicated surgery. Being out of practice, he was most glad that he didn't have to do anything but observe. Once finished he went back to clean with the doctor who said that was the last one that he had for the day. And he was so looking forward to getting home.

Later that night after that surgery floor was closed, he went back to it. He shined a pocket flashlight to the floor and remembered where he had earlier seen everything, in O.r. 7 and 9. Each had the steel box that opened from the sidewall. It was released from overhead; there was no back to this wall. The only space was for it to be dropped from overhead. He got in to trace it by lifting an overhead ceiling panel then stood on a stool to gain access to the crawl way. He crawled all the way to the end of the hospital sidewall. The space around the covered tube had become increasingly smaller. He stopped breathing in ever so little as to not expand his lungs in the much-needed room for space. He hit a wall that was impossible, it had to travel from somewhere, and it couldn't just appear magically from a wall. The only choice was up or down. He calmed his racing mind with logic to figure out what to do.

The answer was void, he then thought down is hell up is heaven-life comes from heaven; he thrust his body upward, success another long tube to follow through. After overwhelming minutes that seemed like hours passed by, he was able to jump down to a larger space being free from what felt like being trapped in a snake. There was no more light, though darkness remained he adjusted his vision and followed a route that leads to a doorway. With fear and apprehension, he opened it. Lighter through a complex woven planned route, he found that he was in unit B of the neighboring storage facility.

He took off his eyeglasses then said to himself, homer's Quest. Being aware of the alarms, he disabled them, and then left the B unit. Quickly sprinting to the unit at 32, got in the white van and drove to the exit. At the locked gate, he got out, opened it with the key, and sped away with the sound of the alarm blasting through the air. He stopped at an Arco station, parked the van in the back then went inside, and bought himself a bag of Fritos and a Pepsi. He enjoyed these as he waited for a cab to take him back to the hotel.

# Chapter 42

T HE NEXT MORNING Troy entered the office of the storage unit to check in with Larry. He was more than surprised at not seeing Larry's bitter face behind the counter, instead, an elderly heavyset blonde-haired white woman stood behind the counter. He stood looking at her in surprise. She said "Good morning" to him, he replied the same. "I see that you look a bit confused. I am sorry to inform you that last night, Larry passed- on. The office informed me to give you this note." She handed it to him, he opened the envelope, and then opened the letter to read it before he could start to read it, she responded to him. "All of his things have been boxed up and I was told that you would take them, once again I'm sorry." He read the note, and then looked confused by it. He took the set of keys from his pocket and took off the company jacket, then placed them on the counter. She looked questionably to him. "It seems that the company has fired me. I left everything here for you. Goodbye." He took the boxes, then got in his Jeep and left the grounds without looking back.

Back at the house Bond sat fully dressed, hair combed, shoes on watching the local news station. He heard the Jeep drive-in; Troy then came in and explained what had happened. Bond told him not to feel too bad about it, now he could just go back to being the movie star double, a life that he enjoyed. He smiled, and then went back to his casita leaving the boxes on the floor of the entry.

The news station then broke into an instant flash news update. The F.B.I. had just been called to investigate an illegal organ transferring at the Valley View hospital. He turned off the television hearing the front door open. "Chris." He stood there; dark wavy hair flowered black background Hawaiian short- sleeve shirt, white canvas shorts and sandals. "You don't want a ride to the airport with me, do you?"

Bond stood up and grabbed hold of his already packed suitcase waiting by the side of the front door. Chris grabbed a hold of Jonathan's boxes. "He's alright, isn't he?" "Yeah, he's already on-route back to the Island" "Were you that doctor?" Chris nodded his head then replied, "Yes," "Glad that you are better brother." "Yeah, it is good to see you." "Chris, uh, are you driving?" "If you want a ride I am driving" They took off to the airport in the convertible Mustang. "Jane will surely be glad to see you." "She sure will." Bond laughs then they both do.